ALSO BY KERIS STAINTON

If You Could See Me Now

KERIS STAINTON

bookouture

Published by Bookouture
An imprint of StoryFire Ltd.
23 Sussex Road, Ickenham, UB10 8PN
United Kingdom
www.bookouture.com

ISBN: 978-1-78681-232-2
eBook ISBN: 978-1-78681-231-5

To Kirsty Greenwood for being awesome.
And for Harry Styles. He knows why.

CHAPTER ONE

I'm standing next to the door in the conference room while Trevor, our CEO, tells us that Fancy Bantams, our biggest and oldest client, is looking for a new agency. They're putting it out to pitch, which means other agencies will try to win their business too, but they're giving us a chance to pitch as well, just in case we can come up with something 'fresh'. Trevor has said 'fresh' at least five times already and he's only been talking for a couple of minutes.

'I want everyone on this,' he says, gesturing around the room. 'I'm determined to keep this client and show them exactly what they're looking for.' He stares at us all and then corrects himself. 'No. Show them what they don't even know they're looking for.'

He pauses for a second, eyebrows raised, as if he expects us to applaud this pearl of wisdom. Everyone just stares at him.

'And as you all know,' he continues, 'Mel's been Senior Planner on this account for, well, years.'

He turns to Mel, my immediate boss. She's got the Mona Lisa look on her face that means she's about twenty seconds from completely losing her shit. If I was Trevor, I wouldn't be standing so close.

'And while Mel has done an absolutely sterling job,' Trevor says – he smiles at her, but I can see the fear in his eyes – 'I feel that this is an opportunity for something… fresh.'

Mel almost snarls.

'I met with Jolyon at Fancy Bantams yesterday,' Trevor continues. 'And his plan is to… *crowdsource* the agency.'

Mel's top lip curls.

'What that means,' Trevor says, 'is that a number of agencies will pitch to the entire Fancy Bantams workforce and they will vote – yes, vote – on the winner.'

Mel rolls her eyes. I must admit, I feel a bit eye-rolly myself. Depending on who actually works for Fancy Bantams, putting it out to a vote could be a Boaty McBoatface-style disaster.

'So what I thought would be interesting would be if we approached it in a similar way here, in-house,' Trevor says. 'If all of the Senior Planners and Planners could work on this account, perhaps we could come up with something fre—' He stops and clears his throat. 'Outside the box.'

Oh, that's even worse than 'fresh'.

'The winning pitch will result in a promotion and/or a bonus, depending on whether it comes from a Planner or Senior Planner,' Trevor says, categorically not looking at Mel, who's turned a startling shade of puce.

'So!' he claps his hands. 'Please all fuck off and do the research and come back with something brilliant. Yes? Yes!' He claps his hands again and we are dismissed.

There's a flurry of chatter as everyone leaves the conference room and heads for their desks. I didn't have time for a tea before I left the house this morning – I didn't sleep well last night and I couldn't get up when my alarm went off – so I head for the kitchen instead. It's not actually even really a kitchen, it's more a corner of the main office, sectioned off with room dividers. I hunt in the cupboard for peppermint tea while I put a mug underneath the hot water tank.

'Hey,' Alex says, stopping in the doorway when he sees me. He smells slightly of smoke, like he's just come in from a smoke break, even though it's early.

I smile at him. 'You haven't seen any herbal teas anywhere, have you?'

Alex is an intern and I'm pretty sure Mel gets him to make her tea all the time. I haven't really talked to him much before – we basically just smile at each other when I see him smoking outside with Nichola, one of the other Junior Planners.

'Not in here,' he says, the corners of his mouth turning down. 'But I do have a secret stash…' He grins.

I raise my eyebrows. 'Mel's?' I mouth.

He nods. 'I shouldn't get you one, but…'

I smile, leaning back against the cabinets. 'I wouldn't want you to get in trouble.'

'I'm a rebel,' he says. 'Wait there.'

While he's gone, I take the mug of hot water and empty it into the sink. I'll make a fresh one when I get a teabag.

'Ta-da,' Alex says, but quietly, which makes me laugh. He's holding a large wooden box, like a chest. Inside are rows and rows of different individually wrapped teabags.

'Bloody hell,' I say.

'I know,' he whispers. 'You know you've made it when you've got your own herbal tea chest.'

I grin at him as I run my fingers across the top of the teabags, trying to decide which one to try.

'I can personally recommend the liquorice,' Alex says, putting the chest down on the counter and cracking his knuckles. I wince.

'God, no,' I say, half-lifting out a raspberry and vanilla. 'That sounds horrible.'

'Also, I'm not supposed to drink these, so forget I said anything,' he says.

I laugh and lift out one labelled 'chocolate and mint'. 'Chocolate tea?'

'I'd steer clear of that one,' Alex says. 'I've heard bad things.'

'I think I'll go classic,' I say, taking out a plain peppermint. 'Thanks so much.'

'So, Fancy Bantams, then?' he says, leaning against the door jamb. 'Ready to come up with something…' He does air quotes. '"Fresh"?'

I grin. 'I don't know. I mean, I'll give it a go, obviously. But I don't fancy my chances.'

'Why not?'

'I've applied for Senior Planner before and not got it.' More than once, I don't tell him.

'Ah, but this is different,' he says. 'This is democratic. May the best pitch win and all that.'

I nod. 'I guess.'

'That's the spirit,' he says, smiling.

I laugh. 'Actually I'm thinking herbal tea's not up to the job today. I'm going to go out and get a coffee. Want one?'

He shakes his head. 'No, thanks. I don't drink coffee.'

'Wow. How do you, you know, stay awake?'

He grins. 'Clean living.'

'God.'

He smiles at me for a second and then looks down at the box of teas. 'Shit. I'd better get this back in the safe.'

On the way to Gino's, the coffee place a few doors down from the office, I think about last time I applied for Senior Planner. How Mel told me that my work was fine, but 'fine isn't really good enough for Senior', how I had to really 'stand out and shine', how I was more of a 'quiet asset' to the company. I'd wanted to smush her non-fat muffin in her face.

'Hey, gorgeous!' Gino's son Marco says as I walk in, his face breaking into a huge smile.

Marco is nice, he is. But he only seems to be able to communicate with women via flirting and it makes me uncomfortable.

Because I'm an idiot, it took me a while to work out exactly what it was about him that made me uncomfortable, but then he asked for my number and winked and the penny – finally – dropped.

'Hey,' I say now. 'How are you?'

He tips his head on one side. 'Better now, darling.'

I do a stupid nervous little laugh. 'Could I have a latte, please?'

'To take away or will you stay with me?'

That laugh again. 'Take away, please. Busy at work!'

While Marco makes the latte, I stare at the chiller cabinet and the pile of muffins. One has a tiny flag with 'salted caramel' printed on it. I can resist a lot of things (actually, I can't), but salted caramel isn't one of them.

Marco turns back with my latte in his hand and one eyebrow raised.

'Could I have a salted caramel muffin too, please?'

'Good choice,' he says.

I rummage in my bag for my purse while Marco bags the muffin and then I hold out a tenner, smiling.

He takes my money and turns to put it in the till, before turning back to me, a smirk on his face, his hands empty.

'My change?' I say.

'You didn't give me the correct money?' He pulls a fake-looking confused face.

'You know I didn't,' I say, my cheeks heating. 'I gave you a tenner?'

'Ah,' he says, smiling. 'I think you're right.' He turns back to the till and takes out some money, but clenches it in his hand and hides his hand behind his back.

'How about a kiss?' he says, twinkling at me as if this is charming and not horrifying. I want to say, 'What the fuck?' I want to say, 'Fuck right off.' But I don't. I do the stupid laugh again and say, 'I really need to get back to work…'

Marco's still got his hand behind his back and now he's pursing his lips. I should tell him to give me my money and fuck the muffin. I glance around to see if there are other customers who might like to comment on how inappropriate this is, but there are only two people in the cafe – a youngish guy in a suit, hunched over his table and talking urgently into his phone, and an older woman with a newspaper spread out on the table in front of her and a biro in the corner of her mouth like a cigarette. She looks at me and rolls her eyes, so that's something.

'Can you please just give me my change?' I say.

He leans forward and taps his cheek with his index finger and, fuck it, I lean across the counter and kiss him on the cheek.

'You want to go out with me,' he says in my ear, before I can pull back. 'I'll treat you really nice.'

'I've got a boyfriend,' I say. 'But thanks.'

All the way back to the office I curse myself for kissing him. What was I thinking? Why didn't I tell him to shove his inappropriate advances right up his arse? Because I didn't want to make a scene? How fucked up is that? I think of all the times men have made me uncomfortable and I let them because I didn't want to embarrass myself, or them. Or my mother. And it makes me furious.

Also, why did I tell him I had a boyfriend? Just 'no' should have been sufficient. I shouldn't need to prove I 'belong' to someone else.

Back at my desk, I Google Fancy Bantams and click on their website. It's quite simple – black, white and grey, clean lines. Very post-Apple. The only interesting thing about it is the logo, which is, inevitably, a fancy bantam. It looks sort of like the Nando's logo, but a bit more over the top. The chicken – is a bantam a chicken? I don't know, I should probably find out – has one leg kicked out like he (she?) is heading off for a stroll. Its face is turned to one side so it looks like it's looking at me, but with just one eye. It's kind of cheeky, but also a bit disconcerting.

I click through to the photos of the clothes. They're all boring. Basic leisurewear in grey, white, black, beige. Cargo trousers, t-shirts, cardigans, hoodies. Not a single thing you wouldn't see in a normal menswear range. The models are thin and pale and bored-looking, standing straight on to the camera and then to the side, like fashion mugshots. I run my hands back through my short hair. Every item is described as unisex. But why does unisex basically mean men's stuff that women can wear? I make a note on my yellow legal pad. It just says 'blah'.

I read the 'About' page and the page about the company's ethics and how the company came about and it's all so bland and worthy that it leaves me wanting a little snooze. No wonder they think it all needs sexing up. But just thinking that makes me feel a bit sad and wrong. Yes, sex sells – it's one of the first things I learned when I started at Houghton & Peel – but why should that be? Shouldn't that be something we work against as we evolve? I know instantly that some of the pitches will focus on getting sexier models, making the women look like they've rolled out of bed and pulled their boyfriends' clothes on, and the men like off-duty boyband members. But edgier. 'Edgy' and 'sexy' should be the keywords for this pitch, I know. But I can't bring myself to do it.

I need something better. Something 'fresh'. Something brilliant. Something to blow their little chicken minds.

CHAPTER TWO

'So,' I say, downing the last of my martini to really build the tension. Not that Tash has noticed – she's more used to my complaints about my mother or the lift at the flats being out of order than anything truly scandalous. 'When I got home last night – I didn't leave work till half eight – Max was watching porn and wanking.'

'In the lounge?' Tash asks, and the fact that this is her first question makes me laugh so much some of the cocktail dribbles down my chin.

'Nice,' she says as I wipe it off with the back of my hand.

A waiter appears next to our table – it's one of the high ones with stools we both had to clamber onto and which I will probably fall off – with another frozen margarita on a round metal tray. Tash flutters her eyelashes at him and takes it, accidentally-on-purpose letting her finger graze the top of the glass so she can lick the salt off it. I look at her – eyes wide, index finger in her mouth – and then I look at the waiter. His mouth is actually hanging open. I wouldn't be at all surprised if a bit of drool came out. To be fair to him, Tash is gorgeous. Beautiful, curvy, sexy. Her dad is from Sri Lanka, so she has this incredible golden skin. Plus she's got huge boobs.

'Excuse me!' I call as the waiter walks – or rather staggers – back towards the bar.

He turns back to me with a look of impatience. 'Another martini for me, please,' I say. 'You know, if you don't mind.'

'Yeah,' he says, still pretty much slack-jawed.

'You are shameless,' I tell Tash. 'And yes, it was in the lounge. Is that better or worse?'

She pulls a face. 'I just don't think it's that big a deal. I mean… do you never watch it together?'

'No!' I say. 'God, no.'

'You don't want to?'

I shake my head. 'I really don't.'

'You don't want to watch porn or you don't want to watch porn with Max?'

I groan. 'I don't know. I don't really want to watch porn. And I really don't want to watch it with Max.'

'Sometimes it's hot,' Tash says. 'Watching together. Sometimes if I get home late, Rob's already watching and I just—'

'La-la-la,' I say, putting my fingers in my ears.

'Very mature,' Tash says. She waits until I pick up my glass and says, 'Suck him off. I just suck him off.'

'Thanks for that,' I say, pulling a face.

I sip at my drink before remembering I've finished it and I try to picture me and Max on the sofa, watching porn together. But all I can see is me in my cloud print pyjamas, Max in his tracksuit bottoms and some band t-shirt, eating crisps and grunting, while I make sarcastic comments about the actors.

'You could try it,' Tash says. 'He might like it. God, you might like it.'

'Maybe,' I say, thinking, *no way*. 'Do you do it on your own? Watch porn, I mean?'

'Yeah,' she says. 'I mean… not all the time, but it's good if I want to get off quickly.'

'Right,' I say. 'And how did it go with…' My mind's gone blank.

'Liam,' she says. She wrinkles her nose. 'I don't know. He's hot. But he's pretty thick.'

'Ah,' I say. Tash and Rob have an open relationship. Apparently. I don't begin to understand it, but she says it works for them.

'But he's also, you know, pretty thick.' She gestures at her crotch.

I pull a face. 'You shagged him?'

'Blew him. In the cab.' She grins.

'Bloody hell.'

'Yeah. He one hundred per cent wants to see me again.'

'I bet he does. What percentage are you?'

She screws her mouth up and looks up at the ceiling. 'Eighty, if I can just go round to his for a shag. Forty if he wants to go out first.'

The waiter brings over my martini, but stares at Tash the entire time. Without looking at him, she picks up a peanut from the bowl in the middle of the table, pops it in her mouth and licks her fingers. The back of his neck's gone bright red.

'What's with all the—' I stick my index finger in my mouth and suck.

'They love a bit of finger action,' Tash says. 'You know they all secretly want a finger in the arse. Did you never see Kanye's tweet?'

'I don't follow Kanye. And they don't,' I say. 'Do they?'

'Well I've never had any complaints,' she says.

'God,' I say. 'I can't imagine doing that to Max. Do you think Max wants it?'

'Oh god, yeah,' she says, grinning. 'Gagging for it.'

'Maybe I should… suggest it,' I say.

'Fuck no. Don't do it unless you want to do it. Do you not think you might like it?'

I shake my head. 'I mean… I've seen his pants.'

She shudders. 'What about if he did it to you?'

'I… no. I don't think so.'

'Surely he's tried it with you.'

'He's prodded around there, yeah, but not with his finger.'

'They're all obsessed,' Tash says. 'But don't knock it till you've tried it. But you haven't said how you feel about it.' She does her American therapist voice: 'How did seeing him wanking and watching porn make you feel?'

I bite at my bottom lip and pick up a handful of peanuts. 'It made me feel… like I don't really want to be with him any more.'

'Seriously?' Tash says, her eyes widening.

'Yeah. Because… I didn't feel anything.' I swap the peanuts to my other hand and take a swig of my drink. 'I wasn't angry or upset and I certainly wasn't turned on. I was just… *meh*. Don't say "I told you so".'

'I wasn't going to,' Tash says, looking at me over the salt-crusted edge of her glass.

'No? You're not going to say he was never right for me? I could do better? I should never have let him move in with me?'

She shakes her head, her long dark shiny hair swinging gently from side to side. For fuck's sake.

'What then?'

'I'm just wondering… Maybe it's not him. Maybe it's you.' She sits back and stares at me.

'Oh god, thanks! Way to blame the victim! How can this possibly be my fault?'

She shakes her head. 'Come on, Izzy! It's textbook!'

I realise I've crushed the handful of nuts almost to powder so I drop what's left of them back in the bowl and wipe my hand on my jeans.

'I don't get it,' I say.

'First of all,' Tash says, gesturing at the bowl, 'gross. Second of all, yesterday I bought myself some new underwear.'

'O-kay,' I say. 'Good for you.'

'It was expensive. It's lacy and black and very sexy.'

'Are you coming on to me?' I say.

I hear a glass smash behind the bar.

'Rob worked late last night and by the time he got home I was asleep. So I put it on for him this morning and I was an hour and a half late for work.'

'Put your back out?' I say. 'Locked yourself in the loo? Caught them on a doorknob?'

She shakes her head. 'He couldn't resist me.'

My glass is empty again, so I reach for hers and take a large gulp. 'Thanks for sharing. That makes me feel so much better.'

'Did Max ever find you irresistible?'

'Are you trying to make me cry?'

'It wouldn't make you cry. Because you're not arsed about him either. Tell me though – does he ever want to rip your clothes off?'

I wince. 'He's not really a clothes-ripping-off kind of a person. I don't think I am either, to be honest.'

She raises one perfectly arched eyebrow. 'Come on. Max did that girl in the bathroom at Jake's party that time when you two were still flirting feebly with each other. I don't think they went in there to watch a couple of *Friends* repeats and then do it missionary.'

I shake my head. 'I don't know why I ever tell you anything.'

She grins. '*Friends* repeats are not foreplay.'

'At first it was a bit more…' I pick up some more nuts and try to remember a time when we really went for it. I'm struggling.

'We had to leave the cinema once. We started kissing – the film was really boring –and we both got a bit… you know. And he said "Shall we just go?" and so we left. And went back to mine.'

'And the sex?'

I can't remember the sex.

'It was good!' I say.

'You can't remember it,' she says.

'Oh god. Tash! Everyone's not like you. I'm not like you! I'm just not that…' I lower my voice, 'into sex.'

'I don't believe you.'

I roll my eyes. 'I don't care. I'm telling you, when we don't do it, I don't miss it.'

She pretends to cough and says, 'Bullshit.'

'I don't!'

'You masturbate, don't you?'

Unlike me, Tash has not lowered her voice. I can't bring myself to look, but I'm fairly confident that the bartender is just leaning on the bar now, watching us.

'I don't want to talk about this any more,' I say. 'Not here anyway.'

'You're repressed. And you're blaming Max. You settled for him because you were scared out there.'

'Out where?'

She waves her arms, knocking over my martini glass. 'Out there! In the world. As soon as Max showed a bit of interest, you sighed with relief 'cos you could stop shaving your legs and start changing into your pyjamas when you get in from work.'

'You don't change into your pyjamas when you get in from work?'

'I do if Rob's away. But if he's there I make an effort.'

'And it's worth it?'

'It is so worth it.'

'And you don't ever get bored?'

'With sex?' Tash looks completely astonished. 'God, no. If you're bored, one of you is doing it wrong. With you and Max? It is probably both of you.'

'Great. That's helpful. Thank you.'

'You're welcome. You need someone who sees you. I don't think Max has ever really seen you. He sees, I don't know, a cheap place to live.'

'Ouch.' I stare down at the scratched wooden edge of the table. 'You don't think he was into me at all?'

She runs one manicured finger around the edge of her margarita glass. 'Do you? You know what I think?'

'I'm about to.'

'You don't want a real relationship,' she says, frowning. 'It scares you. So you sabotage yourself. You've been the same with your job.' I'd told Tash about the Fancy Bantams pitch on the way to the bar. 'You're in. But you're not all in.'

She leans her chin on her fist and stares at me. 'You know I'll help you with the pitch, right?'

I look down into my drink. 'Thanks. I just… I'm not sure I can do it.'

'You can,' Tash says.

I know without looking at her she'll be giving me her Hard Stare. Like Paddington by way of Margaret Thatcher.

'I mean, it doesn't really matter,' I say. 'I'm fine where I am. Assuming the company survives. I heard someone saying that if we don't get the pitch then we're in trouble.'

'No,' Tash says. 'No. You always do this. You always undervalue yourself. You always have.'

'I don't,' I say, even though I know I do. 'I just know what I'm capable of and—'

'And it's much more than you're doing now, Iz! God, you're so frustrating!'

I shake my head. This evening was meant to be fun. I wanted a laugh with my best friend, not a therapy session and character assassination.

'Promise me you'll think about it, at least,' Tash says. 'And I don't mean think about it like "Oh I don't think I can do it", I mean properly think about it. Like a person.'

'God, all right,' I say and I sound like a bratty teenager even to myself.

'And don't mention it to your mother,' Tash says.

She knows me much too well.

*

In front of the restaurant, I stand at the edge of the kerb and hold my arm out for a taxi, while Tash explains to the barman that she's got a boyfriend and no, she's not interested in a bit on the side (mostly because she's already got one) and no, she won't take his phone number just in case. I can't hear them, I just know how these conversations go. She has them practically every time we go out. It's all part of the fun for her. I don't know how she can be bothered, really.

A taxi sails past me, its yellow light glowing. It's one of those evenings that's still almost light, even though it's pretty late – the sky is royal blue and the air is still just warm enough that I'm not worrying about not having a coat with me. I do want to get home though, my feet are killing me.

Another apparently available taxi passes without stopping.

'For fuck's sake,' I mutter under my breath.

I wave frantically in case the driver sees me in the rear view and turns back, but no. Another cab rounds the corner and doesn't seem to notice me either. I look down at myself. Am I invisible? What's the problem? Maybe it's 'cos I'm wearing black?

'What was wrong with that one?' Tash says, joining me at the kerb.

'Didn't see me, apparently,' I say. I lift one foot out of my shoe and wiggle my toes. The middle one is numb. 'And I could ask you the same thing.' I smile.

'Huh?'

'Got rid of your friend?' I gesture back towards the restaurant.

She laughs, wrinkling her nose. 'He was very keen, bless him. Think the wank chat got to him.'

'I'm not surprised.' I grin.

'Don't think I didn't notice that you didn't answer.'

'What?' I lift my other foot.

'Please tell me that you do!' She grabs my arm.

'Do what?' I see another taxi in the distance. I try to make it speed up and stop in front of me with the power of my mind. It doesn't work, unsurprisingly.

'Do… you know.' She wiggles her middle finger at me.

'Eww, Tash. Come one. I don't want to talk about it.'

'It's good to talk about it. And you still haven't said if you do it. You do, right?'

'Sometimes,' I say.

'Good.'

She steps closer to the edge of the kerb, lifts her arm and a taxi in the distance seems to speed up and then skid to a stop next to us.

'Jesus Christ,' I say.

'You take this one.' She kisses me on the cheek. 'I'll get the next.'

I glance back at the restaurant, wondering if she's maybe going back for a drink with the barman. I bet she is. She can't resist them when they're all starry-eyed over her.

'Are you sure?'

'Yep,' she says and wafts her hand. 'Off you go. And I know I was hard on you tonight, but you can do so much better than Max. You need someone who really sees you. In all your awesomeness.'

She kisses me again, pulls open the taxi door and I climb in, banging my knee on the door as I always do. As the driver pulls away, I look back at my best friend. She's still standing there and two taxis have stopped next to her.

On the way home, I think about what Tash said. About me being scared out there. Of course I was scared out there. Dating is scary. And for some reason I only ever seemed to attract weirdos. Like the taxi driver who asked me out and then, even though I said no, sent me flowers, then came round and dropped off a mix CD – a mix CD! – of love songs, and then just waited outside for me one day. To ask me to my face why I didn't want to go out with him. As if I was going to be won over by the creepy stalking and a collection of nineties R&B.

Then there was the client at work who came in for a meeting and seemed really nice. As I showed him out of the office, he asked me for my number, and I gave it to him (even though I wasn't sure if that would be frowned upon by Mel). About an hour later he texted me just one word: *Nudes?*

There was the guy who sat opposite me on the train home to visit my parents. He seemed normal. He spent most of the journey reading a book, ate his sandwich from the buffet without any disgusting noises or spitting, answered the phone and went out into the bit between the carriages to have the conversation. And then, just before the train pulled into Hastings, we started chatting. I can't even remember how, now – something the conductor had announced, I think.

We met for coffee the following week and he was still normal. We met for dinner a few days later, still no red flags. He was a good kisser. He didn't ask me for nudes. He didn't wait outside my flat or send me music. I started to get excited. I started to think of us doing couple stuff together: going to B&Q to buy a Christmas tree, cooking at my flat (me holding out a wooden spoon for him to taste… whatever I was cooking), lying on a beach together, squinting at each other in the sunlight. And then we slept together. And he asked if he could piss in my mouth.

I think about what Tash said about me and sex. I must have had that clothes-ripping-off thing with someone, mustn't I? I can't remember it with Max, but there must have been someone who found me irresistible, who couldn't keep his hands off me? No one springs to mind. I bet Tash could tell me stories the whole way home and possibly to the airport and then on a long-haul flight. And then during the taxi journey at the other end.

The only one I can think of is a waiter on holiday who hung around outside the hotel one evening, said, 'Sex?' and then kissed me passionately while running his hands all over my body. But all I could think of was how weird it was that we hadn't even had a conversation, that anyone could have seen us, that I couldn't remember his name – was he Paco from the bar or Francisco from Reception? (It was Paco. We didn't have sex. In fact, I spent the rest of the holiday avoiding him.) The way he groped me did feature in my fantasies for a few years after, only being done by someone I actually found attractive. Like Gary Barlow. (It was a while ago.)

'Been out, love?' the cab driver asks me as we swing off Ranelagh Road on to the High Street and my bag slides across the sticky floor at my feet. I reach down, pick it up and put it on the ripped and stained plastic seat next to me. My head swims slightly. I should have known better than to have cocktails with Tash.

'Drinks with a friend,' I say, without looking up from my phone. I hate being rude, but I'm too tired for a conversation right now. 'After work.'

'What do you do?' he asks. I glance up and see him looking back at me in the rear view mirror and there's no way I can be rude while I'm actually looking him in the eye, so I say, 'Advertising.'

I see his eyebrows raise and I look out of the window. We're just passing the college. Not far now.

'Advertising, eh?' he says and I can't resist glancing back. I catch his eye again. Kind of wish he would spend more time looking at the road and less at me, but okay. 'I always think of that as more of a man's game.'

I let out an involuntary snort of laughter and then shake my head. 'No. Not really. Most of the senior staff are women where I work.'

Of course the absolutely senior staff – the most senior staff – are men.

I stare out of the window, watching the street lights blur through the glass, but then the taxi turns right and there are no lights, no lights at all, and my stomach lurches with fear.

I look back at the driver who is, now, looking straight ahead at the road. Both sides of the street are in darkness. Why's he turned down here? If he'd stayed on the High Street it was a straight run to St Mary's Road where I live. If he goes down here he'll have to turn left and left again and what's the point of that?

On my phone I double click out of Twitter and load the 'call' button. I press nine and then nine again and feel melodramatic and terrified at the same time. Images of the cab driver pulling over and dragging me out of the cab flicker through my mind, but at the same time, I can see myself getting out of the cab and walking up to my flat, my legs trembling as I shake my head with embarrassment at myself.

I'm darting my head from side to side, trying to take in details of where we are in case I have to give a statement to the police at some point. I look at the cab driver again. Should I talk to him? If I talk to him is he less likely to—

'Diversion,' he says.

'What?' I almost shout.

'Can't go by the park. Burst pipe.'

I blink. I'm picturing the pipe my grandad used to smoke. Burst like on a cartoon? All splayed out, his face black with soot?

'On Kennilworth Road. There's been a burst pipe. The whole place is flooded. It was on the news earlier. Stinks.'

'A burst water pipe?' I say, stupidly.

'Sewage, I think,' the cab driver says. 'Fucking hilarious.'

I shake my head. Is it?

'Not for the shops that are flooded with shit, though,' he says. He turns left and we're back on a brightly lit street, much busier than usual, and I look down at my phone, ready to log out of the call screen. It's already gone to sleep.

Because he's come down the road from the wrong direction, the cab driver pulls up opposite the ex-council block I've been living in for the past four years, in front of the pub me and Max used to go to all the time when we were first going out. Can't actually remember the last time we went in there. Or the last time we went to any pub together for that matter. As I'm rummaging in my bag for my purse – I'd usually have it ready, but I got distracted by all the fear – the cab driver's still talking about the burst pipe. It's knee-deep, apparently. Nice. And I can't find my purse.

'Sorry,' I tell him, dumping a bunch of files out of my bag onto the seat next to me. 'It's in here somewhere.'

'No problem,' he says. 'I know what you women are like with your bags.'

My face is low enough into my bag that I can roll my eyes without him seeing. I find my purse and pay him through the perspex window. Once he's given me back my change, I clamber out, and he pulls away, his phone still in his hand.

I head into the shop next to the pub. I really want a tea before bed – my mouth feels rough after the cocktails – and Max never remembers to buy milk. As I'm waiting to cross the road back to the flats, a bloke outside the pub shouts, 'Oi, darling? Come and have a drink?'

I glance over my shoulder. He's one of three blokes standing outside the pub, smoking. I think I recognise one of them – he's wearing a bright white shirt and he's got sunglasses pushed up on his head, even though it's fully dark now.

'I'm all right, thanks,' I call back, holding up the milk like a complete idiot.

White Shirt looks at his mates – Dirty Jeans and Hipster Beard – and grins. 'Nah, come and have a proper drink. With us.'

I look up and down the street. There's much more traffic than usual, presumably because of the road closure. I could dart out between the cars, but I really don't want to.

'No, thanks,' I call back again. 'But thanks for the offer.'

'Stupid bitch,' I hear one of them say – I think White Shirt but I don't know for sure.

I feel something like pins and needles in my fingers. My stomach curls up and I want to curl the rest of me around it. And then suddenly I'm furious. I picture myself throwing the milk back at them, the plastic bottle cracking, white liquid bursting over that one guy's stupid white shirt. I see myself swinging the bottle hard, my arm extending so that I hit Hipster Beard in his stupid face. But I don't do anything. There's a gap in the traffic and I dart across the road.

I half-expected Max to be asleep when I got in, but no, he's there on the sofa in an Arctic Monkeys t-shirt and his tatty football shorts, playing some video game with cars and guns and screaming. I suppose I should be grateful it's not porn. I just want to make a cup of tea, get in my pyjamas and go to sleep, but as I'm filling the kettle I stop.

What if I tried something different? What if I could really make Max want me? The way Tash said Rob wants her. The way the waiter clearly wanted her. The way Liam, whoever he is, wants her. And we wanted each other at the start, didn't we? We must have done. Maybe that's where we've been going wrong. We let the sex get stale and then everything else got stale as well.

I put the kettle down, and crouch down to look in the small cupboard where we keep the booze we're probably never going to drink. I lift out a litre of Baileys, a bottle of Kahlúa and some sherry I won in a raffle before I see something I actually want to drink: cinnamon vodka with gold leaf. Tash bought it for me and insisted it was incredible, but it sounded gross to me so I didn't even open it. Now I pour myself a tumbler full and knock some back, wincing as it burns my throat. Shit, though. It's actually really good.

When I put the other bottles back, I knock something over in the cupboard and it sets off a domino effect of falling bottles. I flinch, but there's no reaction from Max, which isn't exactly positive, but isn't that surprising either. He seems to have learned to tune out everything that isn't on the TV screen. Maybe he just needs a wake-up call. A sort of intervention. A sexy intervention. I snort and then stop and compose myself. I have to think sexy. And snorting isn't sexy. Is it? I'll have to ask Tash.

I down some more of the vodka and hold the glass up to the light to look at the gold leaf. It's pretty. I don't think I've ever thought about gold being edible. Or drinkable, I suppose. I wonder what happens if you drink too much? I drink some more and then reach round and unzip the back of my dress. I shrug it down so it falls on the floor. That feels a bit sexy, I must admit. But my underwear isn't exactly seductive – it's not my period stuff, but it's not my best either – so I figure naked is probably better. Naked's better for men anyway, isn't it?

I don't know how strong that vodka is, but I think my teeth have gone numb. I strip off everything else and take a couple of slightly wobbly steps towards the sofa. But then I think if I'm going to do it, I might as well do it right. I grab my highest heeled shoes from the corner behind the door where I kicked them off last time I wore them. They're agony. Even squeezing my feet into them now hurts and I worry I'll never get the feeling back in that one toe, but it'll be worth it if it works. If it gets me Tash-level sex. Oh god. I'm actually attempting to level-up sex.

I make my way over to the sofa, trying to do my sexiest walk, which is not actually that easy. You're supposed to walk in a straight line, aren't you? As if you're walking a tightrope. Or you're being breathalysed. I'm a bit too drunk for that. For both. I'm also slightly self-conscious, but not as much as I would have thought because a) I've had cocktails and b) I know this is going to be okay because no straight man is going to resist a naked woman in stilettos offering sex, right? Right.

Max doesn't react as I bump into the back of the sofa, so I steady myself and then slide one hand along the edge, letting my fingers brush against his neck. His head twitches like a fly's landed on him, but he doesn't look at me. Obviously I'm going to have to be a bit more full-on. I swing my left leg up so my foot – in my extremely sexy black slingbacks that are so far working out at seventy pounds per wear – is resting on the back of the sofa. My other leg vibrates with the effort, but I take deep breaths and I'm fine.

Max glances at the shoe – my foot – I'm sure he does. But he doesn't say anything. What's wrong with him? At the very least surely he must be wondering what it's doing there. Maybe he's asleep. I'm not entirely sure how to get my leg back down gracefully, but I decide the best option is to climb over the back of the sofa and on top of Max. He'll have to take the hint then, surely. I mean, that can't even really be considered a hint. A naked woman climbing over the sofa on top of you is hardly subtle.

I move my left leg so my foot is on the sofa cushion and try to slide over the back of the seat. It's not quite as easy as I expected it to be. I end up sort of hoiking myself over with a bit of a grunt and I think I give myself a fabric burn in a delicate area, but once I'm on the sofa – naked, on all fours – there's no question of my intentions.

I crawl seductively towards my boyfriend. My maybe soon-to-be ex-boyfriend who I just want to shag one last time. For science. He's still staring at the TV. But not for long. Surely.

'Max,' I purr, running one hand up the inside of his thigh.

'Do you mind, Iz?' he says without looking at me. 'I'm playing here.'

CHAPTER THREE

Ow, my head. Ow. Ow. Ow.

Ow.

My head.

I'm going to kill Tash. This always happens when I go out with her. Even my hair hurts. And I'm naked. Why didn't I put my pyjamas on or at least a t-shirt? I hate sleeping naked, it's weird. And I wasn't even that drunk, was I? I almost always manage to take off my make-up, clean my teeth and put my pyjamas on. My stomach clenches with panic – did I bring my bag back? I can't remember. I'm not going to get out of bed and check though. There's nothing very exciting in it anyway.

I stretch my legs down the bed and feel a strain in my inner thighs. Shit. Did I have sex? No, I didn't have sex, fuck's sake. Did I? There's definitely a strange feeling... down there. God. I shouldn't be having sex if I'm calling it 'down there'.

Tash didn't have me leapfrogging bollards again, did she? No. I'd remember that, surely.

I open one eye and look at the bed next to me. Empty pillow. No Max. He plays football first thing on a Saturday morning and gets out of bed with more enthusiasm than he has for, well, pretty much anything else.

Oh my god.

Max.

Oh no.

I tried to seduce Max. I roll over and bury my face in the pillow until the image of me flinging my leg over the back of the sofa recedes. Ow. My head. God. The shame. I'm going to kill Tash. This is all her fault. I don't know why I always let her make me feel so insecure. Although she'd say she couldn't make me feel insecure if I didn't already. Or something. But it's hard to feel sexy when you've got a best friend that men – and sometimes women – would merrily knock you down just to talk to.

And I do sometimes think that I want what Tash has. She's right about how I'm lazy, how I'd rather spend the evening in my pyjamas watching *Friends* than shagging frantically in some club loo somewhere. But I do sometimes think that a club loo would be okay every now and again. As long as it was clean.

But of course I couldn't seduce Max. What was I even thinking? That kind of thing needs a build-up, preparation, planning. If I was on the sofa eating Doritos and he staggered over and flopped his knob over the back, I wouldn't be so keen either, would I? But, God, he didn't even look at me. I'd have looked at least. And then said, 'Put that away.'

I curl up in the foetal position. I've felt pretty invisible around him for a while, but that? That was humiliating.

I don't know how much longer I lie there. I cry a bit – the tears running into my ears. I massage my head doing the fingertip Shiatsu thing Tash insists cures all her hangovers. Which is probably bullshit, much like her encouraging sex chat. I reach down and fumble around my inner thighs until I find the source of the pain – a rough bit, feels like a carpet burn, from the back of the sofa. Only I could get a carpet burn without actually getting any sex. Ugh.

Oh god. I can't even bear to think about sex. If Tash thought I was repressed before…

I stare at the ceiling. It needs painting and there's a cobweb the size of a small car in one corner. Everything is shit. I should just stay here until I die. It probably won't be long.

My phone buzzes frantically on the bedside table and after I've said 'Ow' a few more times, I grab it and hold it up in front of my face, head throbbing at the brightness of the screen. It's from Tash. Of course it is.

U get home ok? She's added an emoji with swirly eyes.

Bit bloody late if I didn't, isn't it? My eyes feel a bit swirly, actually. They're certainly not working properly. I screw them up tight, but when I open them again I've got purple dots floating across my vision.

I tap the phone screen to reply, but something's wrong. I can't see my finger. I close and open my eyes again but it's still the same. A migraine. Typical. I had a visual migraine once years ago. That time I had a sort of wobbly water effect in the corner of my eye. This is worse. I can't see my hand at all. What was even in those cocktails? The waiter probably put in double measures in the hope that I'd go home and leave him with Tash. Or he was trying to get Tash pissed and I was collateral damage.

I lift my other hand up, but I can't see that either. What the hell? I can see the phone, but neither of my hands. I put the phone down on the bed then pick it up and try again. No. Phone, but no hands. It looks like the phone's floating in the air. What the actual hell?

I sit up so fast that it makes the inside of my head slide like a bag of shopping in the boot of a car. I grab my temples with both hands and wait for it to stop hammering. While I wait, I look down at myself. I can't see anything. I hold one arm out in front of me. It's not there. I pull the duvet back. Nothing. I can see the sheet, but not my legs.

I'm still asleep. I must be.

I slap myself in the face. Fucking OW.

Someone must have spiked my drink. That would explain the really stupid seduction attempt. That would explain… whatever the hell is going on now.

I carefully swing my legs out of bed and tentatively cross the room to my mirror. Big, free-standing, full-length mirror in the corner of my room. There's no reflection. No. That's not true. There is a reflection of my room. There's no reflection of me.

Apparently I'm fucking invisible.

I don't know how long I've been standing staring at nothing, but I think it's probably been a while. I've been expecting to wake up – obviously, despite the slap, I must be asleep – but no. And then I figured it probably was something in my drink that made me temporarily randomly blind or has given me some sort of psychosis or something, but there's been no change yet. I need to go and drink a huge glass of water, maybe get something to eat. Right on cue, my stomach rumbles and I put my hand on it.

It feels really weird. Not my stomach – that feels the same as usual: softer than I'd like it to be – but it is weird to feel my stomach under my hand but not be able to see it. The amount of times I've stood in front of this mirror naked, grabbing my stomach with both hands. Or turning to the side and sucking it in and then pooching it out. Or looking at my arse and thighs to see whether they've magically shrunk or got any more toned. And now I can't see any of it. Weird.

I put my other hand on my stomach and run both hands across my waist, down over my hips and then up again to my boobs. This is when I would usually hoik my boobs higher, just a couple of inches, so they're pointing forward instead of down. But today I just run my hands over them instead. It feels nice. They feel nice.

But I can't stand here feeling myself up. I need to work out what the hell's happened to me and how I can fix it.

I start by getting myself a glass of water. If this is a hangover – or someone did spike my drink – getting it out of my system is the obvious first step. I pick up a glass and my stomach clenches as I watch it float through the air. It is the weirdest thing I've ever seen. I can feel it in my hand. I can feel my arm moving. But the glass looks like it's moving by itself. If this is a dream it's a really fucking cool one.

Back in the bedroom, I figure I need to work out how this whole invisibility thing works. I've seen TV shows where someone's become invisible and it's as if they're made of glass – they still obviously have a form and you can sort of see their outline. And if, say, they stood in front of the TV, the TV would be blocked, but by something you can't see. But that doesn't seem to be the same for me. I can see through myself.

I stand in front of the mirror again, holding the glass of water I got myself in the kitchen. I can only see the glass. Well, and the water. But I can't see me. No part of me. I drink some, half expecting to see the water travelling down inside my body but a) the water disappears as soon as it touches my mouth and b) the idea makes me feel so disorientated that I have to sit down. I probably need to eat something. I'm getting lightheaded. Or maybe I'm having a stroke?

My phone buzzes on the bedside table. It's Tash ringing, probably because I didn't answer her text. I'm still in front of the mirror, but sitting on the bed, so I see the phone travel up to where my ear should be. Where my ear IS. I just can't see it. Which may be why I hit myself in the side of the head with the phone.

'Hey!' Tash says, when I answer. 'I was starting to worry. Have you only just got up?'

I stare at my lack of reflection. 'Tash. Something really weird has happened.'

'Bad weird or good weird? You sound funny. Are you ok?'

'Sort of. I mean… no. I'm not. But… I was going to say don't worry, but I don't know, maybe—'

'Bloody hell, Iz,' she says. 'You're scaring me! What's wrong?'

I take a deep breath. I can't believe I'm going to say this, but I know I have to. 'I'm sort of... invisible.'

There's silence on the other end of the phone and then I hear Tash snort. 'Jesus, you had me there for a minute. What do you mean? What's he done?'

'No, nothing to do with Max. I'm serious.' I stand up and look in the mirror again. There's nothing to see. 'I know it sounds completely mental. I don't expect you to believe me. But I'm in front of the mirror and I've got no reflection.'

'Like a vampire? Are you hungover?'

'Yes. Well, I mean, I was. I'm fine now. The adrenaline, I think. And I've just had a pint of water. I thought maybe someone spiked my drink...'

'And it made you invisible?' She sounds incredulous, unsurprisingly.

'No, it made me think I was invisible. But, I don't know, it's not getting any better. I'm sitting in front of the mirror now and I'm just... not there. I know this sounds ridiculous, but it's happening, Tash! I mean, it's happened! Really!'

'You're serious,' she says calmly. 'You're seriously telling me you're invisible?'

'Yes!' I flop back on the bed again. 'Can you come round?'

'I'll be there in ten minutes.'

Tash is kidding herself – she lives at least twenty minutes away and that's on a good day – so I decide a shower might, I don't know, wash the invisibility off? I can hear my mum in my head saying 'A bath will make you feel better' whenever I was ill as a kid. She thinks water cures everything. Water and fresh air. And an early night. What the fuck would she say about this? 'Typical Isabel. None of my friends' daughters have ever become invisible. You always have to be different, don't you?' And then she'd suggest a nice silk scarf to set off my lack of visible neck.

It's an incredibly weird experience watching the water running off your body when you can't see your body. But I find that I actually can see my shape under the water. I hold my leg up and the water pouring off it shows me the shape of my leg. I do the same with my arm. It's strangely hypnotic and I bend myself into some ridiculous positions trying to see the rest of me. I manage to see one boob at a time, but I can't do both at once – the water shoots off sideways instead. I close my eyes while I wash myself and almost convince myself it's not real. I can feel my body under my hands, my hands on my body and then I have to stop because it's almost—

'Izzy?' Tash shouts from my bedroom door.

She's got a key to the flat – she's had it for years, since before I even started going out with Max. He used to complain when she let herself in, but he gave up after a while.

'Bathroom!' I call back, turning the water off.

The bathroom door opens and Tash says, 'Are you okay?'

'How did you get here so quickly?' I'm pretty sure I haven't been in the bathroom longer than ten minutes.

'Never mind that now. Are you okay?'

'Do you mean "Are you still invisible?"' I say.

'Yeah. Well. I mean, "Do you still think you're invisible, you knobhead?"'

I pull the shower curtain back and Tash screams.

I look down at myself to make sure she's screaming because she can't see me, not because she can. Yes, still invisible.

'What the fucking fuck, Izzy?!' I don't think I've ever seen her look so shocked. She's usually pretty unflappable.

'I did tell you,' I say, surprisingly calmly.

'I know you did, but I didn't fucking believe it!'

She staggers across the small bathroom and drops down heavily on the loo seat. 'You can't be invisible.'

'I know. But I am. You can't see anything at all?'

She stares at me. Or at where she thinks I am, which is slightly left of where I actually am.

She shakes her head. 'Just sort of… droplets. In the air.'

She's paler than I've ever seen her. Paler than the morning after the night of the Black and White Russians. Paler than the time she saw her ex on the front page of the paper in some dodgy kiss and tell.

'Wait,' I say. 'How about now?'

I pull the shower curtain – it's a crappy white one that cost about three quid in Tesco – up against my body, suppressing a shudder; it's wet, cold and clammy. I tuck it between my legs and wrap the rest as tight as I can.

'Fuck. Ing. Hell.'

'Can you see me now?' I say and then laugh. I must still be drunk.

'Pull it against your face,' she says.

I press the fabric on to my face, poking my tongue out and then dragging a bit between my teeth so she can see where my mouth should be. I mean… is.

'That's one of the creepiest things I've ever seen. You look like a statue come to life.'

'But you can see me?'

'Yes!' she says. 'I mean, sort of. But this isn't even possible. You look like a Weeping fucking Angel.'

'Tash,' I say. 'What the actual fuck?'

CHAPTER FOUR

When I get out of the shower, I wrap a towel around myself without even thinking.

'Whoa!' Tash says, backing up against the bathroom wall.

'What?' I look down. No towel. I hold it away from my body with my hands and it reappears.

'That is seriously freaky,' Tash says. 'So it disappears when it's wrapped around you? Have you tried putting clothes on?'

I shake my head, but then realise she can't see me. 'No. Hang on.'

In the bedroom, I open the second drawer of my chest of drawers and pull out the extra-large t-shirt I usually wear in bed. It's one of Max's old band t-shirts. I borrowed it when we were first going out and never gave it back. I drop it over my head and it disappears.

'So. Weird.' Tash says. 'But then how come I could see you through the shower curtain?' She frowns. 'Should I… Google "invisibility"?'

I roll my eyes. 'I don't know. Maybe. But it's hardly going to tell me what to do about it, is it? I could sort of see myself through the water in the shower too. Maybe you could see me through the shower curtain 'cos it was wet.'

Tash's eyebrows shoot up and she darts back into the bathroom. 'Yes!' she says. 'Wet footprints on the floor.'

I'm suddenly very glad she's here. I wouldn't have thought of that. 'So it's water,' I say. 'Water makes me visible? Sort of?'

'Not visible, but it leaves a trace maybe?'

She comes back in and sits down on the end of my bed. I sit next to her and see her look at the dent in the mattress where I'm sitting.

'Can I touch you?' she says, frowning.

'Um, yeah. Let me just put some knickers on.' I stand up again.

'I wasn't going to touch you THERE!' she says and laughs. Then she flops back on the bed. 'Bloody hell, Iz, how is this possible?'

'I don't know!'

I step into my knickers and watch them disappear. Quite handy really. Don't need to be embarrassed about how greying and saggy they are. I pull a pair of tracksuit bottoms out of my drawer and pull them on too. I usually only ever wear them when I'm on – they're so comfy I almost look forward to that time of the month – and there's no chance of me leaving the house, but it doesn't matter now.

I sit back down and Tash sits up.

'This is really weird,' she says. 'Okay, I'm going to touch you now.' She reaches a hand out and pokes me hard in the left boob.

'Ow! Bloody hell, Tash!'

'Sorry. I panicked. Tell me where you are and—'

I reach out and get hold of her hand, which is still hovering in the air. I can see her hand around where mine should be. 'Can you feel it?' I say.

She nods. 'Have we both gone completely fucking mad?'

'Possibly,' I say and squeeze her fingers.

'You didn't, I don't know, make a wish or anything?' She frowns.

'Oh yeah, that must be it. No, of course I didn't make a fucking wish!'

'Oh god, I know! But I don't know! How can this have happened? Seriously?'

'It can't,' I say. 'But it has.'

*

We do the only thing we can think of to do – make a cup of tea – and sit at the kitchen table while Tash Googles 'invisibility' on her phone.

'This is useless,' Tash says, scrolling.

'We knew it would be,' I say, picking up the tea and feeling the steam tickle my face. 'Because this is impossible.'

'Oh!' Tash says, leaning forward so quickly that she almost jolts the mug out of my hand. 'I saw you then! A bit. Just like a…' She frowns. 'Like a mirage. Do I mean a mirage? It was sort of shimmery and I couldn't really clearly see you. It was like… essence of you.'

'Bloody hell,' I say. 'That doesn't sound completely weird at all.'

'Oh god,' Tash says, pointing at my mug. 'I'm not going to be able to see the tea running through your body, am I?'

I laugh. 'No, I thought that too, but it's fine. Look!' I slurp the tea and then shriek because it's too hot.

'I'd have left that to cool down a bit,' Tash says. 'Invisibility hasn't made you any smarter, I see.' She grins. 'So what are you going to do?'

'Shut your face.' I put the mug down. 'What do you mean what am I going to do? About getting back to normal, you mean?'

'No. Unless you've got some idea about that. You haven't, have you?'

I shake my head. 'No. Not a clue.'

'I meant… It's one of those questions, isn't it?' Tash says. '"What would you do if you were invisible for a day?" So what are you going to do?'

'I'm not going to do anything! I'm going to get back into bed and wait for it to go away.'

Tash rolls her eyes.

'What would you do?' I ask her.

She grins. 'Oh, almost all of it would be illegal.'

'Hey!' I say, remembering. 'How come you got here so quickly earlier? Were you not at home?'

'Ah,' she says, running her hands through her hair and tying it up in a knot at the back. It's one of her signature flirt moves. 'No. I was not.'

'Not the waiter,' I say.

'Why not the waiter? He was cute!'

'He was cute, but he was drooling!'

'Sometimes drooling is good,' she says, giving me one of her sharky smiles. 'And he knew how to drool in all the right places.'

'Jesus Christ,' I say. 'And where's Rob?'

She shrugs. 'Somewhere. I don't know. It's not about Rob.'

'Right,' I say. 'What did he do?'

'Nothing!' she says. 'Honestly! The waiter was cute and Rob is away and I was in the mood…'

'So you're not punishing him for anything? Rob?'

She shakes her head and wrinkles her nose, which I know means she's lying.

'So where is he?'

'He's filming. You know, at that festival?'

'The one in America?' I stare at her. 'Seriously? Why didn't you go?! You said you really wanted to go to that!'

'He didn't ask me.'

'He didn't ask you? Come on! Tash! Why didn't you go?'

She shakes her head. 'I don't really want to talk about it.' She reaches over and drinks some of my tea, even though she said she didn't want one of her own. Her phone buzzes and she pulls it towards her with one finger and frowns at the screen.

'Rob?'

'Liam.'

'Ah.'

She turns her phone over. 'So what are you going to do?'

'I mean it,' I say. 'I'm going to go back to bed and hope I wake up normal.'

'And if you don't?'

'Fuck knows.'

'And what about when Max comes home?'

I shake my head. 'I guess I have to tell him? I mean, I'm fairly confident he wouldn't notice even if I didn't. But if it's… permanent…' I suppress a shudder. 'Then he needs to know.'

She turns her phone over again. 'So…'

'So you're okay to go,' I say, smiling.

'You sure?'

'Absolutely. I'm going to bed. And I'll call you if I need you.'

'Promise.'

'Promise.'

She stands up and holds her arms out and I hug her.

'God,' she says, her breath tickling my ear. 'This is weird.'

'Weirder for me than for you,' I say.

'It'll be okay,' she says, squeezing me. 'I mean, this is impossible. So how long can it possibly last?'

CHAPTER FIVE

Once Tash has left, I'm really not sure what to do. I try to sleep, but my brain is racing with *what?* and *how?* and *the fuck?* and I just can't drop off. I'm also low-key worried about Max coming back and finding me like this. As much as I joke that he wouldn't notice, he'd have to, surely.

I get out of bed and stand in the bedroom doorway. I feel like I haven't had the flat to myself for ages. Usually when Max goes to play football on a Saturday, I go round to Tash's or we go shopping and once a month I go and see my parents. God, my parents. What if this is permanent? How am I going to explain it to them? But it can't be permanent. It just can't.

The flat doesn't even feel like mine any more. The living room – I used to love the living room; it was the reason I wanted the flat, with its huge windows looking out over the rooftops – is basically Max's gaming room. And wanking room, apparently. Although all the rooms are probably Max's wanking rooms.

Tea. I need more tea. And I need to stop thinking about Max wanking. I take my mug over to the kettle. It's got a photo of Max on it – I had it made for him as sort of a joke after our one and only holiday together. We went out on a yacht for the day and I got a photo just as he jumped backwards off the side. His mouth is wide open and his arms and legs are out in a star shape. *We were happy then*, I think, staring at the mug. *Weren't we?*

We were, I think, mostly. I mean, not like all over each other, madly in love, can't bear to be apart happy, but that's not realistic.

But we were happy enough. A few times we were that couple you see sitting at a restaurant not talking to each other – I remember having a row one evening because Max wouldn't put his phone away. We had tapas that night. And then there was the night we tried to have sex on the balcony, but the tile was hard on my knees and I grazed my arse on the plastic chair and Max said, 'For fuck's sake!' And I went back inside, got into bed, and pulled the sheet over my head.

But apart from that, it was good, I think.

We got a really cheap deal and it wasn't somewhere I probably would have chosen – as we were going back to the hotel in the evening, everyone else was heading out to clubs and in the morning we had to dodge piles of sick on the way to the beach. Even so. A holiday's a holiday. I picture us there now, but I can't see us together. I can see me at the pool, but Max is back in the room lying on the bed, playing some game. Do they even have game consoles in hotel rooms? He'd probably take one with him.

I can't picture us out together. When did we last go out together? I can't think of anything. We must have been out for a meal, surely. My birthday? Max's birthday? Christmas? I can't think of anything.

Maybe I shouldn't give up on us. All couples get complacent, I know that, I've read about it in magazines. I shouldn't expect to be jumping for joy at the sight of him, putting on make-up and shaving my legs before he gets home from work, all that crap. But I shouldn't be happier when he's not here, should I?

I take my tea over to the sofa and sit down in front of *Saturday Kitchen*. I'm watching someone from *EastEnders* make an omelette, when a phone buzzes on the coffee table. Max's phone. Next to Max's wallet. He's always been useless at remembering to take his stuff out with him. I'm surprised he hasn't forgotten his keys too. The phone stops vibrating and then starts again and I lean over to look at the screen.

Both texts are from El. I don't know an El. The first says *What time will you be over?* and the second says *Don't shower. I like you sweaty.*

I'm blinking at the screen, trying to work out if there's any way these texts could mean anything other than that Max has been shagging someone else, when a third text pops up.

Can't wait to get your kit off... followed by a football emoji, the aubergine emoji and the water drops.

Unless she's planning to wash his sweaty shorts and make him a moussaka, it definitely seems like Max has been shagging someone else. What a fucking prick.

I'm still sitting and seething – going over the times Max has told me he's been at football or playing pool with his idiot mate Ollie or seeing some band he knows I wouldn't be interested in, and wondering how many of those times he's actually been with her, El – when the front door bangs and Max is back.

I stay very still and he walks over to the sofa and says, 'Ah fuck.' He reaches past me to pick up his phone and then calls out, 'Izzy?'

I want to say, 'I'm right here, dickhead,' but I don't.

He picks up his wallet and takes it with him to the bedroom. I hear him peeing because he never closes the bathroom door. When he comes back through, he's talking on the phone. 'Yeah, babe. I just came back for my phone and my wallet. I got a shower at the gym though. Before I got your texts.'

He's silent for a few seconds and then he laughs, his voice dropping lower. 'I'm sure you could think of another way to get me sweaty.'

I feel something bubbling up inside me and it takes me a couple of seconds to realise it's anger. I don't know how long this has been going on, but it's too fucking long. I grab a cushion from beside me, lift it over my head, and throw it as hard as I can across the room towards Max.

Max's face instantly takes on a 'shocked' expression. He looks like an emoji. His mouth is perfectly round, his eyes wide.

'Fuck,' he says into the phone. 'Something really fucking weird happened. I—'

I reach over to the coffee table and pick up the empty lager can that's been sitting there for a few days now and I throw that too. I aim past him – it's probably about a metre wide – but Max flinches dramatically anyway.

'I've got to go,' he says into the phone. 'What the fuck?!'

I think about throwing the dishes that are littering the coffee table, but instead I just pick them up and carry them across to the kitchen, dropping them into the sink with a crash.

Max's phone is buzzing in his hand, but he doesn't even look at it. I pick up the empty takeaway boxes, the crisp packets, the copy of *The Sun*. I take it all back to the kitchen and throw it in the bin.

I've never enjoyed tidying up quite so much before.

And Max doesn't move. He just watches me carry the stuff across the room. Or rather, from his point of view, watches the stuff float through the air to the kitchen. To him, it must look like the bit in *Mary Poppins* when she clicks her fingers. I click mine right next to Max's ear and he lets out a yell and legs it out of the flat.

CHAPTER SIX

The flat feels strange without Max. Good strange, though. Tash's right, it was more like being flatmates than – and I shudder at the word – lovers. Until, of course, he'd get into bed and nudge his erection up against my arse. Not exactly romantic.

I decide it's time to take back my flat – god knows, there's not much else I can do – and I spend a couple of hours in a frenzy of tidying and cleaning and rearranging. I move the sofa and get all the extra cushions that Max hated back out of my wardrobe. I flip the rug over to hide the mango chutney stain. I change the bedding. I open the windows. I light a scented candle.

And then I pack up all of Max's stuff. Because even though he's only just left (not even left: run away) and even though I may not be in my right mind, I know one thing for sure: I don't want him to come back. Not because I'm invisible and he didn't even notice. Not even because of whoever the hell El is. But because he's always made me feel invisible and I told myself that was okay. It's not okay.

I pack his clothes into suitcases and his gaming crap into boxes and I shove the lot into the cupboard with the ironing board and Hoover and bags and bags of carrier bags.

I flop down on the sofa. I'm flicking through Netflix, trying to decide whether I want to watch a film or marathon a series when the phone rings. My mother. Great.

'Hello, darling,' she says. But with a sigh in her voice. The put-upon sigh.

'Hi, Mum.' I worry for a second that she's going to know I'm invisible through the phone. Do I sound invisible? But of course she's got more pressing issues to deal with.

'I don't know why you have a phone if you never answer it.' She rang me on Thursday, I think. And I haven't rung back. She always says this.

'I just haven't had a chance, sorry. Been really busy at work.'

Another long sigh. 'I feel like we never see you any more!'

Ha. 'I know. I'm sorry. Like I said, work's been busy. We've got this client and—'

'How's Max?'

Ah yes. Zero interest in my job. All the interest in my so-called love life. I think about lying and then I throw caution to the wind.

'We split up,' I say.

'Oh, Isabel!' she almost howls. 'What happened?'

I ponder telling her exactly what happened – *well, Mum, see, I turned invisible, found out Max was shagging someone else, and then used the invisible thing to convince Max the flat's haunted and he freaked the fuck out* – but instead I say, 'It just wasn't working. It's fine.'

Silence.

'I mean… we haven't exactly split up yet…'

Silence. This is what she does.

'But we are going to. We're just not happy.'

'Oh, Isabel, grow up. No one's happy.'

What?

'What?'

'You find someone and you stick with them no matter what. That's just how life works.'

'You're not happy?' I say. 'You and Dad?'

'Oh, we're fine,' she says. 'I just don't understand why you can't…'

'Can't what?' Is it true? Is no one happy? Really?

'It doesn't matter.'

'No. What?' Are my expectations too high? Is that it?

She sighs heavily again and I feel my teeth clenching in response. That sigh was the bane of my childhood.

'You know your father's sixtieth is coming up? Well, he's decided he'd like a party.'

'Mum,' I say. 'You were just telling me that no one's happy and so I should stick with the boyfriend who I don't think I love and who probably doesn't love me. And now you've moved on to Dad's birthday party?'

'Well there's no point talking to you about any of that stuff. I know you're not going to listen. You've always had notions about this kind of thing.'

Have I?

'What notions?'

'About… happiness. And independence. And love.'

Oh. Those notions.

'Is that bad?' I ask her. 'Wanting to be happy and independent and loved?'

She scoffs and I know even through the phone that she's smoothing her hair behind her ears and then fiddling with an earring.

'Not at all,' she says. 'It's just unrealistic.'

It's my turn to sigh. 'So,' I say. 'Dad wants a birthday party.'

'At the sailing club,' she says.

'That sounds good,' I say casually. She doesn't go to the sailing club. It's something my dad does on his own.

'Hmm,' she says. 'Well. He's very keen on the idea. I have no idea why. So can you come?'

Oh shit. How do I keep managing to forget? 'Er. Yeah, I'm sure I can. When is it?'

'You're asking me when your father's birthday is?'

'No,' I say calmly. 'I'm asking you when the party is.'

'On his birthday.' So that's in three weeks. I'll be back to normal in three weeks, won't I? I have to be.

'What time?'

'Eight o'clock. But I was assuming you'd want to get here earlier to spend some time with him. On his birthday.'

'Yeah, of course.' I might just be, you know, invisible.

'And wear something nice.'

'Oh for god's sake.' I can hear teen-Izzy in my voice.

'A dress. Your father always thinks you look nice in a dress.'

'I know,' I say.

And I do know. Last time I wore a dress – to a family christening – he actually took me to one side to praise me for looking 'so feminine'. The 'for once' was implied. And it was a nice dress. But I spent the whole day fiddling with my underwear and trying to stop it riding up. I took my bra off on the train on the way home.

'So I assume you'll be coming alone?' Mum says.

'Probably,' I say.

She sighs again. I'm such a disappointment.

'Sorry to be such a disappointment,' I say.

'Oh, Isabel,' she says. But she doesn't say I'm not.

The conversation with Mum has actually rattled me. I know I shouldn't let her get to me – she's been doing it my entire life, at some point I need to either tell her to knock it off or stop letting it bother me – but I can feel the old teenage feelings coming back.

When she upset me as a teen, I used to go and have a long, hot bath. It was mostly passive aggressive – Mum thinks long baths are self-indulgent and wasteful. She used to have baths in about five inches of warm water until they got a shower put in and now she doesn't have baths at all. But I discovered that if you blocked the overflow with Blu Tack you could fill the bath right up and so I'd spend hours up to my neck in water as hot as I could stand it, listening to loud music and ignoring the fact that we only had one loo and I was stopping everyone else from using it.

I don't bother with the Blu Tack any more, but I do still love a long bath. And I didn't really get to enjoy my shower this morning, thanks to the whole freaking-the-fuck-out thing. I pour in the Molton Brown bubbles Tash got me for Christmas that I've been saving – for what, I don't know – and then I drag the full length mirror in from the bedroom.

I feel better as soon as I sink into the water. I lift one leg and, for a few seconds until the water falls away, I can see it. It's kind of disturbing to watch your own body parts disappear, but it's also so nice to see them again that I don't mind. Once I feel fully relaxed, I dunk my head under the water then stand up and look in the mirror. For a second I can see my whole body. And then it melts away and I feel a bit faint. I grab the shower curtain for support. I don't know whether it's watching myself disappear or standing up so quickly out of a hot bath, but I sit back down carefully and rest my forehead on the edge of the tub.

Shit.

I have got to make sure I'm visible again by the first weekend of next month. I can't possibly attend my dad's birthday party invisibly. But how?

I only get out of the bath when Tash turns up with a takeaway. I've topped up the water repeatedly and I can feel how pruned I am even though I can't see it.

'How was Liam?' I call from the bedroom as she's dishing up at the table.

'Good actually,' she says. 'He's got an amazing body. Six pack, "v" lines, fucking phenomenal shoulders.'

I don't think I've ever slept with someone with a good body, I realise. Max's was okay, but certainly no six pack or 'v' lines, and the only distinguishing thing about his shoulders was that they were hairy.

'I don't think I've ever slept with anyone with a good body,' I tell Tash as I join her in the kitchen.

She rolls her eyes. 'Of course you haven't.'

'What's that supposed to mean?'

'You like to keep your standards low,' she sings, scraping what looks like tikka masala on to a plate.

'That's not fair,' I say. Even though it probably is.

'And just because someone's got a good body, doesn't mean they're a good person!' I pull a dining chair out and sit down. 'I'd rather have a nice person with an okay body.'

'But Izzy,' she says, holding a bottle of Kingfisher towards the middle of the table. I reach out and take it from her. 'You didn't even have that.'

'Text him,' she says, half an hour later, when we've migrated to the sofa with another two bottles, half the naan and some leftover sauce, and I've told her about the texts and the football kit sex and the fake haunting.

'I can't dump him by text,' I say. 'We've been together for two years.'

'I mean… he's been fucking someone else. And you can't dump him in person, can you?'

'You make a good point.' I rub my hands over my face. 'I should ring him, though, right? At least.'

'Go for it. Rip off the plaster.' She laughs. 'The bastard. Rip off the bastard.'

I phone him. It goes to voicemail. And I leave a message.

'I think you know this isn't working. And I think it's time to end it. I've packed up your stuff, you can collect it any time.' I'm about to hang up, when I add, 'This is Izzy.'

Tash laughs so hard she spills her bhuna.

CHAPTER SEVEN

Tash stays the night and only makes approximately three hundred jokes about sharing a bed with me when I'm invisible. I'm so happy she's here, though. If it's possible, this whole thing would be even weirder and harder to deal with without her.

When I wake up, I have a few moments of normal stretching and wondering about the day before I remember – invisibility. And Max. But mostly invisibility.

I stick my arm out above the duvet, squinting into the bright light, but it's not there. At least, I don't think it's there. I get out of bed and cross the room to stand in front of the mirror. Nope. Nothing. Still invisible. Shit.

I make a tea for Tash and put it on Max's – no longer Max's – bedside table. She's got the duvet pulled almost entirely over her head; just a few hanks of her black hair are visible. I pull the duvet back a bit and whisper 'Tea' before heading back to the kitchen and my own tea.

Yesterday, when I was tidying, I made a pile of post on the kitchen countertop, but couldn't be bothered to look at it. Now I sift through it, throwing out an advert for double-glazing, a note from the council about the recycling dates changing and a pizza menu. There's only one actual letter and it's to me, from my bank. Not my main bank, but one that I have an ISA with. My parents set it up for me ages ago when my gran died and I have a standing order paying a little money in each month. You can name the account yourself and I called mine 'Adventure fund', telling myself that once I hit, say, £10,000 I would take some out and go and have an amazing holiday, although Max never fancied any of the places I suggested. If it had been up to him, we'd have gone to Vegas. Luckily, it wasn't up to him.

I slide the statement out of the envelope, unfold it and stare at the balance: £233. They've sent me the wrong statement. Except I already noticed that it said 'Adventure fund'. Maybe they sent me the statement of a stranger who also happens to have an adventure fund? But at the top of the page is my name. My address. And an account number. I have no idea if it's my account number, I don't know it by heart. But this must be a mistake. Of course it is.

I turn the statement over to see the income and expenditure. And there I see my monthly payments going in. Every pay day. Automatically. And the £7500 I expected to see in there going out by bank transfer. I don't recognise any of the details, but clearly I've been scammed. They have insurance for cases like this, though, don't they? You don't just have to suck it up, I know you don't.

My heart is vibrating in my chest and I wonder whether I actually took £7500 out of my own account and then forgot, but I know I need to phone up and ask the question. But it's Sunday. They're probably not even open on Sunday. I turn the letter over. They are. I think about waking Tash up to come and hold my hand, but I am a grown adult woman with a job and a flat. I shouldn't need my hand held to make a fucking phone call.

I dial, my hands shaking. Once I'm through the security questions, I tell the woman on the other end – Scottish accent, very calming – that someone's taken £7500 out of my account.

'Oh dear,' she says sweetly. 'Let me look into that for you.'

I can hear her keyboard clicking and every now and then the phone goes oddly silent and then I can hear the hubbub of the call centre again.

'So,' she says, eventually. 'You authorised a transfer on the 14th February.'

'I didn't,' I say, my cheeks heating.

She makes a humming noise. 'What I can see on the system is that the transfer was authorised with your security details.'

'But it wasn't me.' My chest feels like it's being squeezed. Like I'm being sat on.

'Does anyone else have access to your security information?' she asks.

'No,' I say straight away, but I know that's not true. The letter they sent me with the password and pin number is in my finances file, in the top of my wardrobe. Maybe it's been stolen. I should've checked before I phoned.

'Hmmm,' the woman hums again.

'Can you tell me who the transfer was made to?' I ask her.

'Yes, just a second.'

The line goes quiet again and then there's a click and she says, 'It was to the Halifax bank; the account is in the name M. Coleman.'

I feel like the table is tipping away from me. Or that I'm tipping towards it. I grab the edge of my chair and press my phone harder against my ear.

'M. Coleman?' I repeat. My voice sounds far away.

'Do you have a pen? I can give you the account number.'

'No,' I say. 'No. I don't have a pen.'

I can hear the woman talking as I place my phone down on the table and then put my head down onto my folded arms.

M. Coleman is Max.

Max took all my money.

CHAPTER EIGHT

'Maybe there's an explanation,' Tash says, once I've shaken her awake.

'Seriously?' I say. 'You've never had a good word to say for Max and now you're giving him the benefit of the doubt?'

'I know. I'm surprised too.' She pushes her hand through her hair. 'I just think we should reserve judgement until you've actually spoken to him. He hasn't called back, right?'

'Nope,' I say. 'And now we know why.'

'Hmm,' Tash says. 'Yeah. You should keep trying, though. And maybe use my phone so he doesn't recognise the number.'

'So much for the benefit of the doubt,' I say.

'It's just… There was this girl at work. She had a joint savings account with her boyfriend and she noticed a huge amount going out – like three grand – and she was freaking out because apparently in the past the boyfriend had had a gambling problem, so if it was that she wanted to know. But also she was expecting him to propose and thought maybe he'd taken it out to buy her a ring and that if she asked him about it, she'd ruin the surprise.'

'That's what happens when women are taught to wait for a man to make these decisions. If she wanted to marry him, couldn't she just have said so?' I sip my tea. I think it's the third of the day so far. 'So, which was it?'

'The ring,' Tash says. 'They were married for six months and then she caught him shagging someone else.'

'See!' I say, knocking the bank statement off the table. It skitters across the floor.

'What?' Tash says.

'I don't know,' I say, feeling suddenly weary. 'Men are pigs.'

'Hashtag "not all men",' Tash says. 'But yeah.'

'And I really don't think Max would've bought me a seven-and-a-half-grand engagement ring.'

Tash slides the statement towards me and taps at the transfer. 'He did the transfer on Valentine's Day.'

'Ugh,' I say.

We sit for a few seconds, the silence only broken by me slurping at my too-hot tea and then Tash says, 'What does your gut tell you?'

I automatically put my hands on my belly. I've always hated it, but now that I can't see it, I feel sort of fond. I brush my thumbs over it.

'He took it,' I say. 'The Valentine's Day thing is a coincidence. He never remembered it.'

I don't tell Tash that after I got off the phone to the bank, but before I woke her up, I went to look at my finances file and something was off about it. It was in the same place and nothing was missing, but it wasn't right. Max had been in there, I'm sure. He'd been in there and he'd followed my careful system – colour and date-coded – and he'd found my ISA information and used it to steal all my money. That was really a thing that had happened.

'You're okay for money, though, right?' Tash said. 'You can pay your bills and everything?'

'I don't know,' I say. 'Max paid the mortgage and I paid the bills so I need to check it all out and see what the total is.'

'It'll be okay.'

'I hope so.'

We sit in silence for a few seconds and then Tash snorts with laughter and holds a hand up to her nose. 'Ow.'

'What?'

'I just thought of something. I told you to rip off the bastard. But the bastard ripped you off.'

I stare at her.

'Too soon?'

CHAPTER NINE

'I can't believe I'm doing this,' Tash says, sitting on the sofa, curled over a mug of coffee. 'I can't believe we're doing this.'

She stayed again, I still haven't heard from Max, I'm still invisible. And now it's fucking Monday. And not just fucking Monday, five a.m. on fucking Monday.

'I don't want to change my mind,' I tell her. I've got a towel wrapped round me and another around my head and I'm trying to find something half-decent to wear. 'Mel's been on this account for twenty years. If I'm going to come up with something fresh, I need to see everything that's already been tried. I need to know what worked, what didn't work. I need the full picture.' I lean over, take the towel off my head and rub at my hair.

The best thing about being a Planner is that I can work remotely. Trevor wasn't being hyperbolic when he told us to 'fuck off and come back with something brilliant'; I can literally stay out of the office and no one will care. But Fancy Bantams is such an old client that their original case files aren't online.

I push my damp towel in the washing machine – which is full; probably why I can't find any decent clothes – and then realise that Tash can't see me anyway, so force the towel I've had wrapped round my body in there too. I must remember to put a wash on when I get back later.

'Found anything yet?' Tash says, crossing to the kitchen and putting her coffee cup in the sink.

'Not really.' There's a pile of clean knickers on top of the dryer, at least. 'It doesn't matter though, does it? No one's going to see me. And if I suddenly reappear in the middle of the office, I don't think they're going to be focusing on my outfit.'

'Fair point,' Tash says. She heads into the bathroom while I pull leggings and a hoodie out of a drawer. I pull my hair back in a ponytail, find my trainers under the bed and I'm good to go.

We decide to walk to the office. Mostly because both of us need to clear our heads, but also because we figured we wouldn't be able to talk on public transport. If we're walking we'll have passed people before they have a chance to realise Tash is talking to no one and there's a voice coming from nowhere.

Even though it's so early, there are still lots of people around and I keep seeing people looking at Tash, but it really doesn't bother her that they clearly think she's talking to herself. She's used to people looking at her. And I'm used to feeling invisible next to her.

And I'm actually loving not having to worry that people are looking at me. I've always been self-conscious, I don't know why. Tash says it's my most irritating quality. I used to wish I could be invisible when I was a kid – is that why it's happened now? Some sort of satellite-delayed birthday wish? But it was honestly a relief not having to straighten my hair or put on make-up or worry (much) when I couldn't find anything to wear. I'm not even holding my belly in. It feels really good.

Tash stops for coffee, but obviously I can't get one. A takeaway cup bobbing through the air on its own would attract attention. I'm gasping, though, so once we've crossed over into Dean Street, I ask Tash if I can at least have a sip.

'Bloody hell,' she says, holding her coffee out as if she's feeding a baby from a sippy cup.

Two blokes in low-slung jeans and black vests walk past and one says, 'Alright, tits?' to Tash. I look at her over the top of the cup, but she just rolls her eyes.

'Wankers,' she mutters.

'I could be flashing them right now and they wouldn't even know,' I say.

Tash snorts. 'You're not, are you?'

'No,' I say. 'Bit nippy.'

She rolls her eyes again – at me this time – then announces, 'Nothing to see here! Just giving my imaginary friend a slurp of coffee!'

I laugh, squirting coffee both back at Tash and up my own nose. I cough as Tash wipes the coffee off her jacket.

'God, even invisible you're still managing to show me up.'

And then her face turns serious. 'Shit, Iz, I can see you!'

I feel for a second like the pavement is sliding away under my feet. 'What?!'

'God, not properly. You haven't – you know. But I can see bits of you where the coffee splashed. Wait. I could. You've gone again now.'

I open and close my mouth but I can't think of what to say. Because I'm surprised to find I feel relieved.

'Are you still there?' she says, frowning.

'Yeah. Sorry. I… That just freaked me out a bit. I thought I was back, you know?'

'Yeah,' she says. 'Sorry.'

'That's okay. Thanks for telling me anyway. Obviously liquids are the key. If I really need someone to see me, I just need to throw a glass of water in my own face or something.'

'That'll work.' Tash pats me on what I assume she thinks is my invisible arm. She actually gets side-boob, but I don't tell her.

*

Tash swipes my card into the front door of the building and I follow her inside. That was actually the bit I was most worried about – someone seeing a card swiping itself and the door opening with no one around. Once we're inside the building

I breathe a sigh of relief. We get the lift up to my floor and swipe again to get inside the office. It's early so there's no one around, but the main lights are on – they're always on – and I direct Tash to my desk.

'I don't know how you work like this,' she says, gesturing both at the mess on my desk and the open plan nature of the office. 'God, if I couldn't shut my door and keep the idiots out, I'd never get anything done.'

'It fosters creativity, darling!' I say, quoting Mel.

I sit down and boot my Mac up. I need to copy some stuff to a pen drive first and then we can get the actual files from the archive room.

'Do you want a coffee before I go?' Tash says. 'You've got coffee here, right?'

'Yeah, there's a machine in the kitchen.' I point out the kitchen in the far corner of the room, before realising she can't see me anyway. 'And you've got a caffeine problem.'

'There's a cute boy in your kitchen,' Tash says when she gets back.

I glance at the clock in the corner of the computer screen. It's still only 7 a.m.

'Really?'

'Yep. I just told him I was here with you. He didn't seem entirely awake.'

'What did he look like?'

'Glasses, long hair, big teeth.'

I snort. 'You make him sound like the Big Bad Wolf!'

'He could eat me anytime,' she says, waggling her eyebrows.

'Oh god. Just give me my coffee, you perv.'

She grins. 'Who is he? And why haven't you told me about him?'

'I have, haven't I?' I say. 'Alex?'

'Ah!' she says. 'The Australian? How come you didn't mention he's so hot?'

I shrug. 'I don't think he's so hot. Oh and wait – because you've got a boyfriend.'

'I wasn't planning on marrying him!' she says, rolling her eyes. 'I just thought I might let him throw a prawn on my barbie, climb up my gumtree… or whatever Australians do.'

'I don't think they do that,' I say, still staring at my screen.

'He is definitely hot. You need to take another look,' she says. 'You could stare at him all afternoon and he wouldn't even know.'

'And that wouldn't be creepy at all,' I say.

Tash's phone buzzes repeatedly and eventually she picks it up and checks her messages.

'Oh for god's sake,' she says, rolling her eyes. 'I need to go in. Panic meeting at nine. Can you manage now, do you think?'

'Yeah, I'll be fine,' I tell her.

'You're going to walk back?' She's already putting her scarf back on, getting ready to leave. As much as she moans about her job, she loves it just as much as I do mine.

'No, I thought I could get an invisible Uber. Course I'm going to walk back.'

'Wow, you're narky when you're invisible.'

Once Tash's gone, I download all the files on the local drive, but there aren't as many as I was expecting. I cross-reference the client with the file directory and find that the first ten years' files are actually physical files, not online. And they're in the archive room.

I obviously won't be able to carry them home with me today, but if they're there and easily accessible maybe I could send a courier for them. Or maybe Tash could come again and bring them home for me. I doubt anyone else is going to bother even looking at them, but if someone does want them, I can always send them back.

I can't remember the last time I even had to go into the archive room. All the accounts I've worked on have been relatively new. It's an L-shaped room with shelving down one side and rolling file cabinets at the end. There are no windows and it smells of dust and carpet tiles.

I've only taken a couple of steps inside when I see Alex. He's at the end, standing just to the side of the first rolling file cabinet. He's got an old lever arch file in his hands and he's humming to himself as he scans over the paperwork inside.

I frown as I watch him. I don't know why he'd be in here, why he'd need to be looking at an archived file, but I assume Mel's asked him to find something for her and he's just being very thorough. I should leave – get out before everyone else gets in – but there's something about him. I like watching him.

He's definitely looking for something and he's got a good rhythm going – checking a list on the front of the cabinet, opening the drawer, riffling through the hanging folders, taking out the files. He's quick at it too, although every now and then he takes longer to read something and turns slightly, presumably so the weak light in here shines better on the paper, and when he does that I can see his face.

He's grown a bit of a beard since he started working here a few months ago – more scruff than beard really, but it suits him, even though it's kind of gingery. Actually, his hair is kind of gingery too. Dark ginger. And it's quite long. As he's reading, his hair falls forward and he reaches up and tucks it behind his ear and I feel something clench in my stomach. I'm not sure what it is at first, but then I realise it's just the gesture. It's not something I've ever seen a man do – not that I can think of – and something about it… I have to lean back against the wall.

Alex carries on checking the files and I carry on watching and in the time it takes him to do the rest, I've studied every bit of him I can see. He's wearing jeans and he's got a very nice arse and strong-looking thighs. I bet he's got 'v' lines. I wonder if he plays football. Do Australians play proper football or just that Aussie Rules thing? Although the Aussie Rules players wear really short shorts, don't they? I try to picture his legs in really short shorts and then I drag my eyes back up his body. He's wearing a black jumper with the sleeves pushed up. He's got nice forearms. When he flicks through the folders, I can see the muscles move. He's got nice hands too. Short square fingernails. Clean, which is important. He's wearing a silver band on the middle finger of his left hand.

Finally he straightens up and clasps his hands behind him to stretch. Under his jumper, I see his shoulder blades move and the jumper raises just enough that I see a narrow strip of skin. He's moving towards me before I even realise and I hold my breath and close my eyes as he passes. The air moves and flutters over me.

He closes the door behind him, and I slide down the wall and sit on the floor.

What the hell was that?

CHAPTER TEN

'Lust,' Tash says. 'That was lust. I'm surprised you didn't recognise it.' She pulls her hair back into a ponytail then lets it drop down her back. 'Actually, no I'm not.'

'But I was in his interview! I thought he was nice and every-thing – and obviously he's nice-looking – but I didn't… you know.'

We're back at my flat. It was easy enough to let myself out of the office and walk home, and Tash came over straight from work.

'Get the horn?' Tash says, from the other end of the sofa. 'That's 'cos you're a professional.'

'No, I didn't even think of it. Honestly.'

'You must've done. I think of it with every man I ever see.'

'You do not.' I stare at her.

'Of course I do! I look at their lips and wonder whether they're good kissers. I look at their fingers and wonder whether they know how to use them…'

'Everyone, though? Not just men you fancy?'

'No, everyone.'

'You've met my dad!'

Tash snorts with laughter. 'He's got lovely hands, your dad.'

'Oh my god! You are sick and wrong!'

'I'm serious though. I mean, not about your dad.' She raises an eyebrow in my direction. 'This is normal behaviour. Fancying someone isn't something to freak out about. Honestly. You've just forgotten what it's like because of Max.'

'But I fancied Max!' I say, although I'm wondering if that's really true. And he still hasn't returned any of my calls, the dick.

'Did you, though?' Tash says. 'Really?'

She gives me that look again. She knows me too well. It's annoying. I try to think. I did fancy him, I'm sure. At first. A bit. Enough.

'Did your loins burn when you saw him naked?' she says dramatically.

'Um, no. Wouldn't that mean I had cystitis?'

'Did you want to rip his clothes off?'

'Only when he'd spilled stuff on them.'

Tash laughs. 'Seriously, though. Did you ever think "God, I just have to have you right now?"'

'No. When we did it, I enjoyed it. Mostly. But I was never gagging for it.'

'Yeah, you see, that's the problem.'

'I don't think it's normal, though, is it? That level of… interest?'

She wrinkles her nose while she thinks. 'I don't know. I don't think that level of disinterest is normal, though. You should want each other.'

'You and Rob want each other, but you still want other people.'

'Yeah. Sometimes. So?'

'So I don't get it. If you fancy each other so much, and you like each other… You do, don't you?'

She nods.

'Well then, why sleep with other people?'

She shrugs. 'Because I like it. It's exciting. The one thing you lose when you commit to someone is the first times. First kiss, first touch, first sex. I love all of that. And I don't want to lose it. As long as me and Rob are both cool with it, what's the problem?'

'But are you both cool with it? I don't know how you could be. Don't you get jealous?'

'Yeah. But that works too. It turns me on when he tells me about stuff he's done with some other woman.'

'God, really?' I try to imagine Max telling me about shagging some other woman and me actually liking it. 'I don't get it.'

'No, I know you don't. And that's okay, I don't expect you to. But I still think you should expect more than you had with Max. What was your first kiss like with him?'

'I don't remember it,' I say. 'I was drunk.'

She rolls her eyes. 'Okay. So how about… did you ever feel about Max the way you felt about Alex today?'

I think back to the way I felt after Alex left the archive room. My legs were trembling, my belly was doing a weird hot melting thing and there was a sort of twanging in a… place. I couldn't even focus on looking for the files, I just got the pen drive from my desk and legged it out of there.

'No.'

'There you go!' Tash says. 'You need to shag him. Perfect rebound sex.'

'I think you're forgetting something.'

'Yeah, not now, obviously. Although invisible sex might be hot…' She stares into space.

'Tash!'

'Yeah sorry. I mean once you're back to your corporeal form… or whatever the expression is.'

'If he's interested.'

'Well yeah, obviously, but you could make him interested.'

'Could I?'

'Seriously, you're a grown woman. You've had boyfriends, you've had sex, you just need to… do it better. Expect more. Of them and of yourself.'

'How?'

'You need to practice. You know. On your own. That works. 'Specially now Max has gone. Do stuff you like. And if you don't know what you like, work it out. Buy some smutty books. Or watch some stuff online. Really think about it. And don't worry if it's weird or kinky. No one can see you anyway. Perfect time to find your, you know, Sex Mojo.'

'Hmm,' I say.

I tip my head back and look up at the ceiling. I'm not sure I've ever thought about that. What I want, I mean. That can't be true. I must have done. But I can't remember. With Max it was always pretty much the same. And the men I slept with before too. Bit of nipple-bothering, quick fiddle about to see if I was ready and then it was all about them. Fuck.

'You know what I just realised?' I say, deciding to file the bad sex away to think about some other time.

Tash quirks an eyebrow at me.

'I've never had a proper first kiss sober.'

She frowns. 'Seriously?'

I nod. 'I don't remember most of them. I absolutely haven't had the whole romance novel "his hands on my face, he looked into my eyes, our lips touched" thing.'

'Fuck me,' she says. 'That's the saddest thing I've ever heard. I mean, it's not always like that – I've had first kisses that were messy and our teeth bashed together or it was too hard… I split some guy's lip once – but they've all been memorable, at least.'

'I'm starting to wonder if I've actually wanted to kiss any of the men I've kissed,' I say quietly.

'Jesus Christ,' Tash says. 'I need more wine.'

'Do you want to stay over again tonight?' I ask, getting up to go and get another bottle.

'I don't think you're ready for this jelly,' she says, grinning.

'Piss off,' I say, laughing. 'I just meant… Rob's still away, right? Or have you got plans with someone else?'

'I was thinking about maybe seeing Liam, but I can totally just sext him, he'll love that.'

I walk out to the kitchen, come back with the wine and top up both of our glasses. Tash shuffles up the sofa towards me and turns her phone around, holding the screen up in front of my face. There's a photo and at first I can't see what it is, but then—

'Oh my GOD, Tash!'

'Nice, innit?'

'Why? Why would you show me that?'

'If you're going to start dating again, you need to know your way around a dick pic.'

'Jesus.'

'I can get him to send a video later, if you want.'

'I've changed my mind,' I tell her. 'You should go home. Or maybe to church.'

Tash smirks. 'You know, this could be just what you've needed all along.'

'What?'

She wafts her hands in my direction. 'You know. Your predicament.'

'Being invisible is what I've needed all along?'

Tash sighs and rolls over, looking up at the ceiling. 'You've always sort of felt invisible anyway, right?'

Now I sigh too. 'Right.'

'So now you really are, you're free. To do whatever you want. You don't know how long it's going to last, so go mad. Live on the edge. Diddle yourself into next week.'

'You've got such a way with words.'

Tash grins. 'That's why I'm in PR, baby!'

'You know what I need to do?' I say later, when we've finished the second bottle of wine. Tash has started on the third and even though I've switched to water, my words aren't coming out of my mouth quite as clearly as they should be. 'I need to kill that pitch.'

'Yesssss!' she says, swinging her wine glass towards me, the wine almost but not quite sloshing over the top. 'You totally will. You're so good!'

'But how can I?' I ask. 'I mean, I'm invisible.'

Tash nods, her face suddenly serious. 'You are. Invisible. But you probably won't always be.'

'Probably,' I say.

'So if you're not invisible then you'll be able to do it.'

'Or maybe not,' I say. ''Cos it's hard.'

'Lots of things are hard,' Tash says. 'That's no reason not to even try.'

'No,' I say. But I'm thinking, *Isn't it?*

'And you can do it, of course you can. You're so brilliant. You should be doing more than you are! Everyone knows that.'

'You always say that,' I tell her. 'But it's not true.'

'It is!' she says, slamming her glass down on the coffee table. The wine jumps up and settles back down again. 'I don't know why you're thinking it's not. I don't know why you always think you're…' She stops. Frowns.

'What?' I say. I have no idea what the end of that sentence is going to be.

'Not enough,' she says. 'Not good enough.'

'I don't,' I say, but my voice is quiet.

'You do. Not good enough for a better job. Not good enough for a better relationship. Not good enough for…' She picks up her wine again and finishes the glass. 'University,' she says.

I drink some more of my own wine. It's funny, we never talk about that any more. Or maybe it's not funny, it's just understandable because it was ten years ago. But she used to ask me about it a lot. And then she stopped.

'I just… it was so much harder than I'd expected it to be,' I say.

'But why?' she says. She's leaning towards me, a cushion cuddled against her stomach, and she looks genuinely concerned.

'Because…' I look at the bottle of wine and wonder if I could have more. I want more. I pour another glass. 'Because you weren't there.' I close my eyes.

'Ah, love,' she says.

She drops her head down on my shoulder, slightly head-butting me in the jaw, but I don't say.

'I just wanted to get away. From home. From my parents. But it would've been so much more fun with you.'

'It wasn't all bad, right?' Tash says. 'Uni?'

I close my eyes. The main thing I picture when I think of university is of me, alone, in my sad room in Halls. Or my sad room in the house I shared with a group of girls I had nothing in common with. It was the hardest three years of my life.

'I wish I hadn't had to do it on my own,' I say now.

'I always worried,' Tash says, looking down into her glass. 'I always worried that I made it harder for you.'

'What?'

'That I made it harder for you to go to uni. I mean, you said you wanted to go, but I was all "oh no, come to London with me, it'll be fun!" And so that made it so much harder for you. Did I?'

I shake my head. 'No. God. Tash! No. I mean, you did say that.'

We both laugh.

'But I wanted to go to uni. I just wanted to be in London with you at the same time. If I'd got into UCL it would've been fine.' I shudder, remembering the horrible interview I'd had there.

Tash drops a hand from her glass and it lands on my shin. She jumps a bit, then smiles and slides it down to wrap around my ankle.

'I wish I'd put London off and gone to uni with you,' she says. 'I wish you hadn't hated it so much.'

'Same,' I say, even though at the time I told myself I needed to be away from her, out of her shadow, to find the real me. Turned out the real me was much, much happier in Tash's shadow.

'And at least we did live together for a little while,' she says.

I nod. 'Remember the wanker?'

Tash chokes on her wine and I have to wait out a coughing fit.

'Oh my god,' she says eventually. 'Yeah. Horny little monkey.'

He lived above us and would start every single day with some self love. We'd hear the bed creaking and banging, followed by a groan and then the bathroom tap running. I could never quite meet his eye when we saw him in the pub.

'That flat was a proper shithole,' Tash says.

It really was. Small and cramped and beige and damp. But close to the Tube and not too expensive.

'You've gone up in the world,' Tash says, holding her arms out to gesture at my flat.

'You too,' I say and she nods.

'We're both really lucky.'

'Yeah,' I agree. 'Apart from the whole invisibility thing.'

'Yeah,' Tash says. 'Apart from that.'

CHAPTER ELEVEN

I wake up with a crick in my neck and freezing cold feet because Tash is the world's worst duvet hog. It's just starting to get light – the room has that watery, early morning feeling. I stretch my legs to the end of the bed, feeling my hips and back crack, my muscles resisting and then relaxing. I put a hand behind my neck and massage the soreness out and it's only then that I think to check if I'm still invisible.

You'd think it would be the first thing I'd think of when I wake up. But no. And it doesn't even feel that urgent to check. It's only been three days, but I'm already sort of used to it. Which is ridiculous, I know. But it's still true.

I hold my hands up in front of my face. And they're not there. Or rather they are, but I can't see them. Okay. Something between nerves and excitement flutters in my stomach and I'm not really sure what to do with it. Surely I don't prefer being invisible? But I have to say, it's a lot easier. I don't even have to shower if I don't want to. (But I probably should.)

It's only when I roll onto my side that I realise the other side of the bed is empty and there's a piece of paper on the pillow. It's a leaflet about a new local hairdresser's, but in the inch of space at the top, Tash has written *realised had to go home before work, ffs. Call me if you need me. Being invisible hasn't made you snore any less*, and then she's drawn a smiley face with the tongue sticking out.

*

In the shower, I watch my body under the water and smooth my hands over the skin I can't see. It feels nice. My body feels soft in some areas and strong in others and I think about how, in the past, I spent so much time focusing on what was wrong with it, the parts I felt I should try to change. I don't want to change anything now. My soft belly feels nice under my hands and I think about all the time I spent grabbing it with my fists as if it was dough.

I slide my hands over my breasts, which I always thought were too small, too droopy, but they feel good too. I brush my thumbs over my nipples and feel a corresponding flicker between my legs. I think about what Tash said last night. About learning what works for me, what I like. I can't believe I'm twenty-eight and don't even know. Actually, it's worse than that; it's not just that I don't know, but that I haven't even really wondered. I just assumed that what Max wanted was what I wanted. God.

I really don't want to think about Max right now, so instead I picture Alex in the archive room: his back muscles moving under his t-shirt, his fingers as he flicked through the files. I imagine his fingers flicking through me and lift one leg against the side of the bath to get better access. And then I imagine myself slipping, hitting my head, knocking myself out. Dying, invisible, in the bath. All for a wank. It would make a good TV movie, at least. *Dying for a Wank: the Izzy Harris story.*

I shake my head. I'm being ridiculous. But maybe I should sit down, just in case. I sit under the flow of the water, turned sideways so that I can lean against one side of the bath and brace my feet against the other. I keep my left hand on my boob and move my right down between my legs and gasp, my head tipping back against the wall.

I keep my fingers moving slowly over myself as my thumb brushes my nipple and I think about Alex.

What if I'd crossed the room and put my hands on him? On his hips. Turning him around to face me. In this scenario, I'd be visible, no matter what Tash says. He looks surprised, but his eyes darken when he sees the look on my face and I drop to my knees and undo his jeans. He pushes his hands into my hair as I take his… his… length? God, I've read too many romance novels. Whatever. I put it in my mouth. And I hear him groan and I hear myself groan as my head bangs back against the tile wall and heat pools in the base of my stomach. My legs are shaking and my fingers are cramping, but there's no way I'm stopping. I squeeze my eyes shut against the water beating down on my face and I cry out as I come.

By the time I finally get hold of Max, I've called him seventeen times. And I only get him after that because I finally give in and call his mum.

Max's mum, Jenny, is absolutely lovely. But she's quite hard work.

'Izzy! Sweetheart!' she says, when I get through to her on the phone. 'How are you?'

I wonder what she'd say if I said, 'Well, I turned invisible and your son nicked all my money,' but of course I don't. What I say instead is, 'Not bad.'

'Oh, I know, I know,' she says. 'I was so sorry to hear about you and Max. I was going to send you some flowers, actually. And a little card. But I don't need to now, because here you are! On the phone!'

'That's really lovely of you,' I say.

'Thank you,' she says, as if she actually did send me flowers rather than just thinking about it. 'Max hasn't really told me what happened…' she says.

I recognise this for what it is. Max has told her nothing. Literally anything I say will be news to her. I'm not falling for it. I used to fall for it all the time when Max and I were first together. She'd say something like 'Max tells me you were out for dinner…' and I'd tell her where we'd been, who we'd seen, what we'd eaten and then she'd say something passive-aggressive like 'I can't remember the last time I went to a restaurant,' or 'Isn't it nice how you young people can afford to eat out?' even though she and Max's dad actually eat out all the time and at much more expensive places than we were ever going to. Max's mantra was to tell her nothing. At first I thought he was cold, but I soon came round to the idea.

'Hasn't he?' I say vaguely. 'I was just wondering if you could ask him to give me a ring? I'm not sure if he's been getting my messages, there's a problem with my phone.' The problem is he knows the number and he hasn't got the balls to answer.

'I'm not sure…' she says. 'He's here now, actually.'

'Oh,' I say. 'Right.' I assumed he was staying there, but thought he'd be at work. Why isn't he at work? Maybe he's heartbroken by our split. Or traumatised by the 'haunting'. Or more likely just on a sickie.

'But I'm not sure it's a good idea for you to talk to him,' Jenny says. 'It may be too soon.'

Jesus Christ, I want to say. *He's a grown bloody man. He doesn't need you to protect him from the woman he was living with until last week.* But I don't, of course. Instead I say, 'It's actually pretty important. So if you wouldn't mind…'

'Well,' she says. 'I'll ask him.'

She puts the phone down and I hear her heels clicking across the wooden floor of their kitchen. I can tell when she's opened the door because I hear the unmistakeable sound of Call of Duty on a much higher volume than Max ever had it here. I don't know how the rest of them can stand it.

The Call of Duty sounds stop suddenly and then Max is on the phone, saying, 'Hey,' and I am overwhelmed with anger.

Don't fucking 'hey' me, you twat! I want to say. But instead I say, 'So. We need to talk about some stuff.'

'Shit,' he says. 'Is this about the mortgage?'

'What?'

'Fuck.'

I hear his mum tut in the background. Might've known she'd be hanging around, trying to find out what I've phoned for.

'Hang on,' Max says.

I hear something that sounds a bit like a scuffle. Max has covered the phone so it's muffled, but I can hear his voice and his mum's voice much higher and then Jenny's back on the phone.

'Max is just going to take this in the study,' she says. The study is the second bedroom. There's a desk in the corner.

'How's the family?' Jenny asks.

I try not to laugh. My mum and Jenny are very similar. Before they met, I thought this meant they would get on well. Both of them were extremely keen that 'the parents' should get together. My mum went on and on at me, Max's mum went on and on at him. Finally my parents were coming to London for a show – a matinee – and so I suggested we all have dinner together afterwards.

Our mums were delighted. Until they actually met. They did not get on well. We had one dinner with the four parents, during which our mums talked to each other through gritted teeth and Max's dad downed about six pints of lager while my dad scoffed his way through a plate of fish and chips the size of a buffet centrepiece. No one ever suggested meeting up again.

Max once let slip that his mum refers to my mum as 'that woman'. Usually that wouldn't bother me at all – my mum's a pain in the arse – but because it was Jenny it got my back right up.

'Hey,' Max says again, presumably once he's in the study. Lying on the bed, no doubt. 'Sorry about that.'

'What about the mortgage?' I say.

'I lost my job,' Max says.

'What? When?'

'March,' he says.

It's June.

I open my mouth to speak but I have no idea what to say.

'I've been looking for another one,' Max says. 'But I couldn't sign on—'

'What? Why not?'

'Because I quit. I mean, I had no choice. So I thought it'd be okay. But they don't let you sign on for, like, twelve weeks or something.'

'Right,' I say. There's a rushing sound in my ears.

'So I didn't have any money coming in. Basically.'

'You haven't been paying the mortgage?' My chest feels tight. I rub it with the heel of my hand.

'Only since March,' Max says.

'Oh!' I say sarcastically. 'That's absolutely fine then! The mortgage company lets you not pay for a quarter of a fucking year!'

'Seriously?'

Jesus Christ.

'No! Of fucking course not! God, Max!'

There's a silence, in which I wait for Max to apologise, confess about the ISA and whoever the fuck El is, beg my forgiveness, but no go.

'So,' I say eventually. 'Are you going to tell me about the ISA?'

'Yeah,' Max says. 'Um…'

'Um?' I actually hold the phone away from my ear and stare at it, like there's going to be a little 'WTF?' lit up above it. 'Seriously?'

'I didn't take it,' Max says.

'You did, though,' I say.

'Yeah. What I mean is. I loaned it. To Michael. He was meant to get it back to me and I would've put it back in your account and you wouldn't even have known. I mean, he still might.'

'What?' I say. My head feels light and weird. Like it's filling up with fog. 'You gave it to your brother?'

'Yeah. He needed money for something. Like an investment thing. He was going to get more back and it was only meant to take a couple of weeks, but something got fucked up and—'

'I can't believe I'm hearing this.'

'I know. I know it sounds bad—'

'It *sounds* bad? All my savings are gone, Max! It *is* fucking bad!'

'He still might get it back. Some of it. He thinks.'

I lean forward and rest my forehead on the table.

'And what am I supposed to do in the meantime?' I ask Max.

'Can't your parents pay?' he says.

'I...' I lift my head slightly and let it drop down onto the table, but I fail at knocking myself out. 'Forget it,' I tell him.

'If I get it back—' he starts to say.

'Yeah,' I say. I can't feel my hands. 'Yeah. Whatever.'

'I'm... sorry,' Max says slowly. 'About the money.'

And everything else? I think. But it wasn't just him. I let him stay because it was easier to. We both fucked up. There's no point even mentioning El. He doesn't know that I know. And I don't care.

'Thanks,' I say.

'If I get it back, I'll ring you,' he says.

'Yeah, that would be good,' I say. 'Thanks.'

'I need to collect my stuff too,' Max says.

'Yeah,' I say. 'I've packed it up so whenever you like, really.'

'Great,' he says. 'Thanks.'

'No problem,' I say. 'See you.'

I end the call and lean back on the chair, still worrying at my thumb. I've got a sliver of nail caught between my bottom front teeth and I try to dislodge it with another nail.

It's so weird that Max and I were together for two years and this is how it's ended. And that I'm not even upset. I don't feel anything at all. How can I have loved him enough – or even liked him enough – to live with him, to spend so much time with him, to sleep with him, have sex with him, and not even care that it's over? I just feel… nothing.

That's not true, actually. I feel relieved. That I get another chance to be with someone. To find someone I really want to be with. My stomach flutters at the thought.

CHAPTER TWELVE

The next morning I head into the office early again. My plan is to grab the files I need, leave them on my desk and then send a courier to collect them. No idea how I'm going to sign for them, but I'm hoping Tash will be able to come round and do it. Plus I can take photos of the relevant bits on my phone and be in and out of there before anyone else is even up. Even opening the door with the swipe card shouldn't be a problem at this time of day, as long as I keep an eye out for street sweepers or drunks on the walk of shame.

Walking to work is lovely. So lovely that I tell myself I'll keep doing it, whatever happens. It feels like London is just waking up – the sun is turning the buildings warm and golden. The streets are wet from the street cleaners and every cafe and coffee shop I pass smells delicious. It's easy to take this city for granted, I think, particularly when I get in the habit of getting the Tube to work and home again without really stopping to look around – but today I do stop and look around and it's wonderful.

There's no one near my building apart from a homeless guy almost directly opposite, but I think he's asleep and he's got his back to me. I take my swipe card out of my bra – I realised this morning that as long as it was inside my clothes, it wasn't visible – and quickly open the door.

I glance at my desk on the way past, but it doesn't look like anything's changed. Alex's black jumper is hanging over the back of his chair and I actually think about stopping to sniff it before telling myself to get a grip. It'd probably smell of smoke anyway. I notice he's got a copy of H.G. Wells' *The Time Machine* on his desk. I like a man who reads. Max didn't read anything that didn't have a red top or a 'busty lovely' on the cover.

Trying to remember why I went out with Max in the first place (*Because he asked*, a voice in my head says. I ignore it), I make my way to the archive room. I think I thought opposites attracting was a real thing. Or maybe I just wanted it to be. Or maybe it was because he was friends with the guy Tash was seeing at the time and I liked the idea of double-dating. I don't know.

As I pass the kitchen, I realise there's someone in there. And they're singing. It's a male voice and I recognise the tune, but can't quite place it.

As I get closer, I can hear the singing more clearly and it's so familiar that it starts to annoy me. What is it?! It's when the singer – who I am pretty sure is Alex – starts playing percussion with what sounds like spoons on mugs that I realise a) he's in the kitchen and b) he's singing the Super Mario theme music.

I cover my mouth with my hand as I laugh and step close enough to be able to see him through the open kitchen door. He's wearing a white t-shirt, grey tracksuit bottoms and white socks. He's dancing, his feet scuffling across the lino, bum wiggling, as he sings and sort of beatboxes the game sounds.

I blush, thinking about what I imagined him doing to me in the shower. And last night in bed. And this morning just as I was waking up. What I imagined doing to him. I stare at his bum a bit more. Might need to remember that later.

He drops a teabag in a mug and pushes the mug under the hot water tap then sings the sound the game makes when a flower emerges from a block, shoulders shimmying, and I try to smother my laughter again, but I don't quite manage it and a snort escapes.

Alex stops dead and, for a second, doesn't even turn round. He slides the mug out from under the tap and then turns and looks out of the door. I wonder what he's doing in the office so early.

'Is someone there?' he calls. He narrows his eyes and pushes one hand back through his hair.

I want to leave because it feels creepy to be here when he doesn't know I'm here, but I don't want to move in case I bump into something or otherwise alert him to my presence. I stand stock still, breathing as lightly as I possibly can.

He steps closer to the door and leans out, one hand on the door jamb, and looks around the office. His eyes slide straight past me, of course, but I still close my own eyes again, as if that'll help him not see me. I'm such an idiot.

I stay exactly where I am until he's made his drink and gone round the corner to Mel's office, and only then do I let myself carry on round to the archive room.

There are so many Fancy Bantams files archived that there's no way I can take them all home. I hope Mel's filing skills have improved over the years; there's so much irrelevant crap that should never have been filed in the first place, let alone archived. I've got a pile of files to take – I've pushed them under the desk near the shelving to make them less obvious – and I'm reading over the very first brief document from 1996 when something slams into me from behind.

I'm knocked to the ground, dropping the bottle of water I brought with me – it rolls across the floor and something weird happens in my brain. It feels like everything's happening in slow motion. I watch the water sink into the grey carpet and I try to catch my breath.

It's only when I hear him say, 'What the hell?' that I realise it was Alex who crashed into me.

I don't know what to do. If he takes another step, he'll fall over me, but there isn't enough room for me to get out of his way. I roll onto my side and try to crawl under the desk next to the pile of files, but there isn't enough room and I can't properly get underneath it.

'Izzy?' Alex says.

I swallow a gasp and clench my teeth.

'Yeah, course it's not Izzy,' Alex says. 'Idiot.'

I turn my head slightly further than is comfortable so I can see him. His cheeks are flushed and he looks utterly bewildered, unsurprisingly.

'What the hell was that?' he mutters. And then he looks straight at me. And shakes his head. I look down to make sure I'm still invisible – and I am – but he's still looking at me, with a little vertical line between his eyebrows.

'Izzy?' he says again.

I hold my breath.

He crouches down, frowning, and reaches his hand out towards me. And I have no idea what to do.

I panic.

I put my hand out to stop him touching me, but his hand makes contact with mine and he shrieks, jumping backwards. I jump up, forgetting I'm under the desk, and I hit my head. And my face. And I make a noise I can't describe. It's sort of 'Shit' but muffled by a smashed face and a person realising that they really shouldn't say anything at all because they're bloody invisible in their office with one of their co-workers. A hot co-worker.

'Izzy?' Alex says again.

I half-drag myself out from under the desk, putting my hands up to my face.

'What the fuck?' Alex says.

'You can see me?' I hold my hands out and for a second I can see them too. Why can I see them?

'You're bleeding,' he says.

'I'm invisible,' I say. My voice sounds weird.

'Yeah,' he says. 'I kind of got that.'

And then apparently I faint.

When I come round, I'm flat on my back, my head's on something soft, and my face feels cool. I open one eye. Alex is looking down at me, his eyebrows knitted with concern. Or maybe horror. It's hard to say.

'Alex?' I say. It comes out as a croak.

His breath whooshes out. 'You're okay? Thank fuck for that.'

'Am I still invisible?' I say. 'My face feels wet. Oh shit. Is it blood?'

He shakes his head. 'No, no.' He holds his hand up and I see he's got a handful of the paper towels from the bathroom. They're dark green so I know they're wet. Also, his hand is shaking. It makes something twist in my stomach.

'Your nose was bleeding, but not a lot. It's stopped now.'

'But I'm still invisible?'

He nods.

'So how come you haven't run away screaming?'

'I'm Australian,' he says, giving me a shy smile. 'We don't do running and screaming. Although, full disclosure, I might've shit myself.'

I laugh, but stop suddenly when it makes my face feel like it might explode.

'Sorry,' Alex says, smoothing the paper towel over my forehead.

Realisation dawns as my head starts to clear. 'And you can see me? A bit. Because of the water.'

'Yeah. So…' He tips his head on one side. 'I should probably ask…'

'How this happened?'

He nods.

'Yeah. I don't know. I just woke up like this.' I picture myself posting a picture with that caption on Instagram – a picture of nothing – and I snort. Ow.

'Seriously?' Alex says, ignoring the snort. 'How long ago?'

'Saturday. So today is day five. I was hoping it was one of those forty-eight-hour things…'

He nods. 'Forty-eight-hour invisibility. I've heard of that.'

I laugh again and feel my heartbeat in the bridge of my nose.

'Why does my nose…' I start to say, but then I realise I bashed my face on the desk. Great.

'So how come I can see you with the water?' Alex asks.

He's left the wet paper towel on my forehead now, but he's gently brushing my hair away from my face. I feel some of the strands tug a little where they've presumably been caught in the blood from my nose. I must look horrifying. Or I would. If I wasn't invisible.

'I don't know,' I say. 'I don't know anything, really. I tried Googling it, but it turns out this is impossible, so it wasn't much of a help.'

'No, I wouldn't have thought so,' Alex says, the corners of his mouth twitching into a smile. 'But you're visible as long as you're wet?'

His cheeks flush pink. The memory of fantasising about him in the shower (and, er, in bed) (and also on the sofa) pops into my mind and I shove it away, feeling my face heating too.

'Seems that way,' I say. 'You can't see me properly, right? Just sort of outlines?'

'You kinda look like you're made out of water, if that makes sense,' he says.

'It's weird, isn't it? When I'm in the shower it sort of looks like I'm melting. Like I'm dissolving in front of my own eyes.'

Why did I mention the shower? I shouldn't have mentioned the shower.

'Do you think you can sit up?' Alex says. 'I'm worried we need to take you for medical attention, but—'

'But how could we do that? I know. I feel like I'm in one of those films where I have to keep away from the authorities 'cos they'll want to do tests on me.'

'Do you feel okay?' He smiles. 'In yourself, I mean?'

I laugh. 'Yeah. Actually, I feel great. I mean, not right now – my nose hurts and I feel like an idiot – but in general, I feel better than I have in years.'

'Right. Okay.' He frowns. 'It's getting late. I think people are going to start arriving soon.'

'Shit, yes. I need to go.'

'Can you walk?' He holds his hand out. 'Sorry, I can't see where…'

'It's okay.' I wrap my hand around his. It feels strong and warm. It still seems strange to me that I can feel his hand even though I can't see mine. But I guess it must feel even stranger to him.

'That's weird,' he says. Then his cheeks flush again. 'I mean, not bad weird, just—'

'I know,' I say. 'Sorry.'

He shakes his head, his hair falling forward from where he'd tucked it behind his ear. 'No, I am. I just didn't expect it to feel like—'

'A normal hand? I know.'

I let him help me up, but even when I'm standing, he doesn't let go of my hand.

'Do you need help getting home?' he says.

'No, I'll be fine,' I say. But then I think, *What if I faint again? What would happen if I fainted and no one could see me?* I shudder.

'Actually. If you wouldn't mind…'

'No worries,' he says. 'Is there anything you need?'

'Yeah. There is.'

'How do I talk to you?' Alex mutters out of the corner of his mouth once we're outside on the street. He's got all the files I need in a box and the weight of them makes the muscles in his forearms flex. I'm trying not to look at them.

I step closer so I'm talking directly into his ear. 'Probably best if you don't, unless you're okay with people thinking you're talking to yourself.'

He smiles. 'I'm not that bothered, tbh.' He actually says 'tee bee aitch'. He steps to the edge of the kerb to hail a taxi that's just come round the corner. It stops right in front of us and Alex holds the door open for me. I climb in and Alex gets in after me.

'Where you going, mate?' the driver asks.

As he puts the box of files on the floor of the taxi, Alex says, 'Er. I've forgotten the address, actually. Just bear with me a sec…'

I look at the rear view mirror and see the driver roll his eyes. Alex gets his phone out of the front pocket of his jeans, holds it up in front of his face and opens FaceTime. Seriously? He's FaceTiming now? Who with?

'Hi!' he says brightly, even though it's still showing the contact screen. 'How's it going, Izzy?'

I open my mouth and close it again. What?

'What was that, mate?' the driver says.

'Sorry,' Alex says, holding his phone out a bit further. 'Just on the phone with my… girlfriend. Getting the address.'

'Ah right, sorry,' the driver says. 'Didn't realise. FaceTime? It's great that, isn't it? My daughter's working in Belize and—'

'Sorry,' Alex says, pointing at the phone and pulling a face and the driver nods and stops talking.

'No, I'm just in a cab,' Alex says, angling his body slightly towards me. 'What's the address?'

'Twenty-two St Mary's Road,' I say quietly.

'Twenty-two St Mary's Road! Thanks! Can't believe I forgot.'

He leans forward and gives the address to the cab driver, then sits back, looking very pleased with himself.

'That was impressive,' I whisper.

He grins. 'I impressed myself there, not gonna lie.'

CHAPTER THIRTEEN

I open the door to the flat and Alex walks in ahead of me.

'Who the fuck are you?' I hear Max say from inside.

'Shit,' I mutter, following Alex through the door. 'Boyfriend. Ex.'

Alex nods and then says, 'Hey, mate. I'm Alex.'

He puts the box of files down on the kitchen table, crosses the room, and holds his hand out towards Max.

As I walk around the table, I see what Max had been doing – disconnecting his Xbox from the TV. I packed up all the games, but I forgot about the actual console. There's a cardboard box on the coffee table and I follow Alex across the room to see what else Max is planning to take.

'I'm not your mate,' Max says, ignoring Alex's hand. 'Who are you?'

Alex glances over towards the door where he obviously thinks I'm still standing. 'I'm a friend of Izzy's.'

'Oh yeah?' Max says. 'I've never met you. What's your name?'

'Alex. I work with her. And we have met, actually. Briefly.'

At first I can't think when Alex means, but then I remember a leaving do in a pub; Max rude and bored, spending the hour or so we were there playing a game on his phone. God.

Max rolls his eyes. 'She never mentioned you.'

'Maybe you just weren't listening,' Alex says.

I look from Alex to Max and back again as they square up to each other. I doubt they're going to actually fight, they're just both doing that thing men do. Puffing out their chests like chickens. Or cockerels, I suppose.

It's funny – they're so completely different in every way. Max is definitely more what I would think of as my type – darker, broader, short hair. I used to love the back of his neck after he'd had his hair cut. If I could think of any example of being overcome with lust, like Tash had asked me, that would've been it – when he came back from the barber's and I wanted to bite the back of his neck.

'How do I even know you know Izzy?' Max says. 'How do I know you weren't breaking in?'

I walk around the coffee table, careful not to bump into anything, and stand next to Alex. I slip my keys into his hand.

'With a key?' Alex says, holding up my Mickey Mouse keyring.

'Why have you got her keys?' Max says. He rolls his shoulders back and pushes his chest out. I know he's sucking his stomach in too – it's hard to maintain a six-pack when you spend every evening on the sofa eating takeaways.

'She gave them to me,' Alex says.

'Why?'

'What's it to you?' Alex says.

'Why should I believe you?' Max says. 'How do I know you haven't mugged her, taken her keys and come here to rob the flat?'

'I've got ID,' Alex says, dropping my keys on the coffee table and taking his wallet out of his pocket. 'Alex Wynne. You can phone the office to check, if you like.'

Max glances at Alex's wallet, but not long enough to properly read or register anything.

'Yeah, okay,' he says. 'I'm just going to get my stuff and go, yeah?'

'Fine by me,' Alex says.

I lean over to look in the box and, as Max finishes winding wires around his Xbox, I reach in and lift my digital radio out.

Cheeky bastard. I see Alex's eyebrows shoot up, but I've put it on the sofa and covered it with a cushion by the time Max has stood back up.

'Okay then,' Max says.

He looks around and for a second I think he's getting nostalgic, that he's sorry for how things turned out, but then he says, 'Good luck with Izzy, mate,' and I have an urge to kick him in the crotch. Alex and I follow him to the door and as he steps out, Alex says, 'Got your keys?'

'Oh yeah, right,' Max says. He puts the box down, takes his keys out of his pocket and hands them to Alex.

'Cheers,' Alex says and shuts the door in his face.

'You could literally have been anyone,' I say, once Max has gone.

'Yeah,' Alex says. 'Nice guy.'

I've said this already, but I still can't get my head around it. 'Seriously,' I say again. 'For all he knows, you could have been planning to wait here and kill me.'

'I know.'

'I mean, seriously!'

'I know!' Alex smiles at me from the other end of the sofa. I'm impressed with how often he does seem to be actually looking at me. He's really good at identifying exactly where my voice is coming from.

'Look on the bright side,' he says.

'I got my radio?' I say. 'The Xbox has gone? I don't need to change the locks?'

'All of those. But I was thinking, you know, you're well rid of him. No regrets over the end of that relationship.'

I laugh hollowly. 'I didn't have any before. But, no, you're right there. I'm counting my blessings, that's for sure.'

'When did you split?' Alex asks.

'I mean… a couple of days ago.'

'So he doesn't know about…' He gestures at me.

I smile. 'No. Well. Sort of. I kind of pretended to be a ghost and he freaked out and legged it. And then I told him not to come back.'

Alex blinks at me and then laughs. 'You pretended—'

'I mean, not literally. I didn't go "woo" or anything. I just moved some stuff around. More like a poltergeist.'

Alex shakes his head. 'Wow. And he didn't notice?'

'What? The stuff moving? Yeah, that's why he—'

'No, I mean, he didn't notice you were invisible?'

'Oh,' I say. 'No.'

'How is that possible?' There's a little line between his eyebrows and I want to stroke it.

I shrug. 'He stopped looking at me a long time ago.'

Alex stares at me for long enough that I start to blush. Even though I know he can't see me. I grab a cushion and pull it against my stomach, watching Alex's eyebrows raise very slightly.

We sit in silence for a minute or so and I picture Max and Alex squaring up to each other again. While Max looked full of bluster, Alex was completely calm. He looked like he had the whole thing under control. And I guess he did. It was impressive.

'So…' I say, breaking the silence. 'Can I make you a cup of tea or something? Or do you have to get back?'

'A tea would be good,' he says. 'Thanks. I mean, if that's okay. I can go if you—'

'No,' I say. 'It's good. I mean, it's fine. For you to stay. A bit.'

'Actually, I'm just going to go out for a cig, if that's okay?'

'You don't have to go out,' I say. 'If you just go over by the window.' I glance over to make sure it's open. It is.

He runs one hand back through his shoulder-length hair. I've never really been into long hair on men before, but it suits him. I like it.

'You sure?'

'Yeah,' I say. 'No problem.'

'So how long have you been over here?' I ask as I fill the kettle. 'I know you mentioned it in your interview…'

'Coming up to a year now,' he says from the other end of the living room.

'And you came over on your own?' I ask, glancing over as I take two mugs out of the cupboard.

'No,' he says. 'Well, yeah. I came to Europe with friends, but to London on my own.' He pauses and adds, 'I was with my girlfriend and my best friend. But then they hooked up, so…'

'Oh god,' I say, closing the kitchen cupboard and staring at him. 'That sucks. How long were you together?'

'Five years.'

'Wow. You must've been young?'

'Yeah. High school sweethearts.' He smiles. He's holding the cigarette right out of the window between drags.

'Did she break your heart?'

He dips his head, hair falling down over his face, and then he looks back up, almost directly at me. It makes my belly flutter.

'She kinda did, yeah. But she was right. I mean, it wasn't right that she hooked up with my best mate. But if she'd tried to break up with me, I probably wouldn't have accepted it. I thought it was really romantic, you know? High school sweethearts, travelling together… I had all these dreams about the two of us living in London. But she knew it wasn't right. She saw it before I did.'

'What wasn't right?'

'We were too young. We hadn't lived.'

'I haven't lived,' I say. 'And I'm older than you. Horrible to lose a friend too, though.'

'Yeah. They're getting married now, though, so, you know, it worked out okay.'

'For them,' I say, dropping the teabags into the mugs.

'And for me,' Alex says, smiling. 'I love it here. Love my job. Love London. Just have a few things to sort and then it'll be perfect.'

'You're not planning to go back?'

He shakes his head. 'No. Not for a while, I hope.'

I pour the hot water into the mugs and reach up into the cupboard for sugar.

'It is really weird watching the tea making itself,' Alex says.

'Oh god!' I say. 'I didn't even think of that. Is it freaking you out? You can totally do your own.'

'No, it's sort of fascinating. I would've loved this when I was a teenager.'

I get the milk out of the fridge.

'Wait,' Alex says. 'That came out wrong. What I mean is I was obsessed with unexplained phenomena when I was a teenager. The Bermuda Triangle, spontaneous human combustion, astral projection, that kind of thing.' He grins. 'Too much *X-Files*.'

He's finished his cigarette and he comes back over to the kitchen.

'Can I just…' He gestures at the tap and then runs his cigarette end under it before throwing it in the bin.

I smile back at him. 'I've always been creeped out by anything like that. I had a friend years ago – sort of an acquaintance, really. You know, one of those people that you think might become a friend? Anyway, a group of us went out one night and on the way back she started telling me about the angels in her bedroom. I thought she was joking at first, but no. She seriously thought she had all these angels lined up in her bedroom, watching over her. She'd given them all names.'

'Maybe she really did.'

'She didn't, though, did she.'

Alex laughs. 'How do you know?'

'Because how could she?'

'You don't believe angels exist?'

'No. Do you?'

He shakes his head. 'No. But only because I've never seen one.'

'You've never seen one because they don't exist.'

'But how do you know for sure?'

'Because it's stupid.'

'Can people suddenly become invisible?'

I actually start to say 'no'. I really do. Instead I say, 'Yeah, okay. But that's different.'

'Because it's happened to you. So you know it can happen. But if you phoned your angel friend and told her you were invisible, would she believe you?'

'I don't know. Probably not.'

'Exactly.'

'Exactly what? You have to experience something to believe it?'

'No. I think you have to keep an open mind. You know the first trains were only allowed to travel at twenty-five miles an hour because people thought heads would explode if they went faster. Genuinely.'

'Hmm,' I say. I squeeze the teabags against the sides of the mugs and then drop them in the sink.

'I'm not saying you have to believe in angels…' Alex says.

I laugh as I add the milk. 'Thanks.'

'But, you know, you wouldn't have believed this either.'

'No. I wouldn't,' I say. 'Sugar?' He shakes his head. 'I still sort of don't,' I say as I carry the teas over to the sofa. 'Maybe none of it's real. Maybe I had an embolism or something and I'm in a coma and this is all a fantasy.'

'Interesting that you think I'd be in your fantasy…' He grins. And then his cheeks go pink.

I try to think of something to say, but I've got nothing. 'Tea,' I say instead, putting the mugs down on the coffee table.

'So you're still planning to do the Fancy Bantams pitch?' Alex says as I sit down.

'Yeah. I don't know why. I mean, if I'm still like this I won't be able to actually do it.'

'Right. Yeah. That could be a problem.' He grins at me. Or towards me.

I don't know what Tash was talking about – he hasn't got big teeth at all. He's got a big smile, yes, but his teeth look perfectly proportioned to me.

'I'm happy to help in any way I can,' he says.

'That's great,' I say. 'I have no idea what I'm doing right now, but if I work it out, I'll let you know. Thank you.'

Even if I'm not invisible any more I'm still not sure I'll be able to do it, but I don't tell him that.

Alex picks up his tea and blows it. I watch the steam ripple over the surface and realise that he'll be able to see me, briefly, when I drink mine. It makes me feel oddly nervous. And also excited. My stomach flutters distractingly.

'I'd love to go to Australia,' I say to take my mind off it. 'Actually, I'd love to go anywhere. I've never really travelled at all.'

'Why not?'

'I've never had enough money since moving to London. I did have an "Adventure Fund" – I was going to get to a certain amount and just take off, but…' I don't want to tell him about Max stealing it. I don't even want to *think* about Max stealing it. 'I bet you've travelled all over, haven't you?' I say instead.

He has the decency to look a bit embarrassed before he starts listing all the places he's been, some of which I've never heard of.

'Yeah,' I say, smiling. 'You've got that backpacker vibe about you. That's why I wasn't sure when you came in for interview.'

'You weren't?' he says.

I laugh. 'Nope. Sorry. I thought you were a bit of a chancer at first. You know, just looking for something to pass the time before you went off on your next adventure…'

He grins. 'I get that. I even thought that at first – when I started looking for a job, I mean. I thought I'd just do it for a few months and then I'd be off again. But I really love London. I'd still like to travel more, though. One day. You haven't appreciated a coffee in the morning until you've bought it from a stall and drunk it sitting on the beach, watching the sunrise.'

I laugh. 'Oh god. You're one of those.'

'One of what?'

'One of those "You haven't lived until you've been off your face on mushrooms in Thailand… You just don't know joy until you've swum through coral…"'

He laughs. 'Oh god. A wanker, that's what you're saying. I sound like a wanker.'

'Only a bit,' I say and pick up my tea. I feel the steam rise up in front of my face and I stare straight ahead, at the spot next to the TV where Max's Xbox was and where now there's just an empty square outlined with dust.

'Hi,' Alex says and I drag my eyes away to look back at him. He's looking at me with the softest expression and it makes me want to run out of the room and hold a pillow over my own face. Either that or push him back on the sofa and straddle him.

'You can see me,' I say.

'A bit, yeah.'

He's still staring.

'I've noticed, though – you're really good at knowing where I am anyway. I think you've got powers.'

He smiles. 'You believe in powers now?' He drinks a bit more tea, then says, 'I can sort of feel you. It's not hard. Close your eyes.'

'Why?'

'Just close them. I'm not going to do anything. I just want to show you something.'

'I've fallen for that one before,' I say. And I hear rather than see him laugh, because my eyes are already closed.

'Closed,' I say.

'Now touch me,' he says.

My breath catches in my throat and heat pools in the base of my stomach. I reach out my hand and immediately know just what he means. Even before I touch him, I can tell where he is. It's sort of like when you put your hand out towards a TV screen and you can feel the fizz of energy in the air.

With my eyes still closed, I slide my hand along his arm and then onto his hip. I drag my knuckles across his stomach and up his chest, hearing his intake of breath. I move closer and trace my fingers up his throat and along his jawline, feeling the scruff of stubble under my fingertips.

'See what I mean?' he says, his voice low.

'I do,' I say, dropping my hand back to my lap.

We're silent for a few moments and I wonder if he's thinking about kissing me. I'm thinking about kissing him.

'I should probably be getting back to work,' he says.

'Oh, right,' I say, blinking. 'Yeah, of course.'

We each walk around opposite ends of the sofa and I stop him by the kitchen table with my hand on his arm.

'Thank you,' I tell him. 'For coming back with me. And everything.'

'No problem,' he says. 'I'll see you in the office?'

'Hope so,' I say.

He smiles. 'Call me if you need anything, okay?'

'I will.'

As we both walk to the door, Alex almost bumps into me and I hold out my hand to steady him. I'm aiming for his elbow, but he moves his arm and I end up touching the back of his wrist.

My fingers on his skin sends a shiver right through me and I feel my breath catch in my chest.

'Bye,' he says at the door.

I close it behind him. Wait until I hear his footsteps on the stairs and then hit my head repeatedly against the wood.

CHAPTER FOURTEEN

After Alex left yesterday, I spent the rest of the day reading the files. I got up early this morning and started on them again, and now I'm finally starting to make some notes that I think actually make sense.

It's taken me hours – I forgot to have lunch and I'm just thinking about making some toast when my phone rings. Tash. Rob's back, so she stayed at her own place last night and I haven't even had a chance to tell her about Alex coming round.

'I've got so much to tell you!' I say as soon as I answer.

'Iz?' she says, and then for a few seconds, all I can hear is sniffling. My stomach rolls with nerves – Tash doesn't cry.

'Tash?' I say, standing up. 'Are you okay?'

'No,' she says. 'I'm not okay.' Her voice sounds strained and weird, like she's been crying for a while.

'What's happened?' I feel sick. What if something really bad's happened and I can't help 'cos I'm fucking invisible?

'Rob… Me and Rob… Can I come and stay with you?'

'Of course. But what's happened, Tash? You and Rob what?'

'He's with someone else.'

There's a thump as if Tash has dropped the phone and then I can hear a hiccup and a sob before she picks it up again. 'Sorry,' she says. 'He's in love with someone else.'

'Oh my god, Tash.' I look around the room as if I'm going to suddenly spot something that will help me deal with this. 'Where are you?'

'I'm at…' There's a long silence and I close my eyes tightly, trying to will her to be okay.

'I'm at a bar,' she says.

'Are you on your own?'

'Yeah,' she says.

'Stay there,' I tell her. 'I'll come and get you.'

'You can't,' she says simply.

'I fucking can,' I say. 'Give me the address.'

I'm standing in front of my building, looking across at the pub where those dickheads yelled at me that night – god, it seems like years ago when it's actually less than a week – when Alex pulls up outside in a black cab. He opens the door, looking over towards the building and I'm so relieved to see him, I feel a bit tearful. I touch his arm gently – I don't want to scare the shit out of him – and he immediately looks almost directly at me.

'Izzy?' he says quietly.

'Hi,' I say. 'Thank you.'

He runs his hand down my arm and takes my hand then clambers back inside the cab, pulling me in with him. I drop down next to him.

'You in?' he asks me, his mouth close to my ear.

I squeeze his hand to indicate 'yes' and he pulls the door closed and then leans in front of me to pull a seatbelt round me.

'Where now, mate?' The cab driver asks.

I look at him. He's looking straight ahead, not back at us in his rear view mirror, which is a relief. Not that I think he'd notice the seatbelt. I'm starting to realise people don't really see things they don't expect to see. And even if he did notice, he's more likely to think Alex is a weirdo than that he's picked up his invisible colleague to go and find her drunk and heartbroken best friend.

My phone is tucked inside the stretchy black vest I've been wearing instead of a bra and I tug it out and show Alex the name and address of the bar Tash is at on my phone. He gives the cab driver the details and gets his own phone out, holding it up in front of his face.

'Hey,' he says.

'Hey,' I say back, quietly.

'You okay?'

He leans against me and I press back against his arm. For the first time since I answered the phone to Tash, I start to feel more relaxed. Less terrified.

'She'll be okay,' he says, before I've replied.

'Yeah,' I say. 'I just… I just want to get to her, you know? Thanks for coming with me.'

'Of course,' he says. 'You couldn't very well go on your own. Although I do think that would be worth seeing.'

I smile, picturing invisible me dragging Tash out of a bar while the men who are no doubt swarming around her look on, confused. When I phoned Alex, he didn't even hesitate. I said I needed help and he just left work and came to help me. I don't know what I would have done if he hadn't.

'Is it far, do you know?' I ask him now.

'Do you know how long it's going to be, mate?' he asks the driver.

'Shouldn't be more than fifteen, if we're lucky,' the driver says, glancing back in the rear view mirror.

'Great, thanks,' Alex says.

'Oh shit,' I say. 'I haven't brought any money.'

'No worries,' Alex says. 'I've got money.'

'I'll pay you back,' I say. 'I promise.'

I turn my head and rest my forehead gently on his shoulder. He smells like smoke, but I'm surprised to find I don't mind it.

'Thank you,' I say again.

I look out of the window and realise we're on England's Lane. Max and I used to come here a lot when we were first going out together. There was a tiny restaurant that did the most amazing pizzas and then we'd go to the pub on the corner and stay in there all night. We were happy then, I'm sure we were. I try to remember if we went home after and ripped each other's clothes off, like Tash asked, but I'm pretty sure we never did. I remember once standing between his legs when he sat at the bus stop and he pushed his hand down the back of my jeans, but I'm pretty sure I told him to knock it off.

I text Tash to tell her we're on the way, we should be there very soon, but she doesn't reply. I carry on staring out of the window and after a few more minutes, sit up straight and lean towards the window when I see some buildings I recognise coming up on the right; three Victorian red-brick mansion blocks near Lord's Cricket Ground. When Tash and I used to come down to London on the Megabus – it was so much cheaper than the train – we'd pass these blocks and always say that one day we'd get a place there together.

Course, we didn't know back then that some of the apartments cost over a million quid.

About five minutes later, the taxi stops in front of a much more modern, much uglier, mansion block and the driver says, 'It's just there, on the corner. I can't get any closer – roadworks.'

Alex leans across me to open the door and then pays the driver as I get out of the cab and wait for him on the pavement.

I wince as I see the workmen in the middle of the road turn in my direction, but then I remember they can't see me. I want to whistle or shout 'Nice arse!' at them, give them a taste of their own medicine, but I need to get to Tash. The taxi pulls away, stopping almost immediately at the lights, and Alex says, 'Izzy.'

'I'm here,' I say and reach out for his hand. He squeezes my fingers and says, 'Let's go and get her.'

The pub is not at all what I've been imagining. In my mind, Tash was slumped over the bar of some seedy dive, her cheek resting in a pool of beer, creepy men circling her while rock music played and a huge hairy barman in leather slowly polished a glass with a tea towel, looking at Tash and licking his lips.

Instead we walk into a bright and modern gastropub. The U-shaped white wood bar is surrounded with mismatched bar stools, the free-standing tables are marble-topped, the booths around the outside of the room are red leather. Adele's *21* is playing quietly and instead of a hairy barman, there's a young-looking woman with a black asymmetric bob, red lipstick and black-framed glasses. She smiles at us and says, 'What can I get you?'

I'm about to answer before I remember she's not smiling at *us*, she's smiling at Alex.

'I'm just looking for a friend, actually,' Alex says. 'I mean. My friend's here. Already.' He frowns.

I spot Tash in the furthest booth in the far corner of the room and tug at Alex's hand.

'Ah!' Alex says, smiling at the woman. And then we're crossing the room and sliding into the booth across from Tash.

She looks terrible. Beautiful, of course, she always looks beautiful, but more miserable than I think I've ever seen her. Her eyes are red and her face is pale and her hands, in front of her on the table, are shaking.

'Oh,' she says, staring at Alex. 'Why are you…?'

She leans down and rests her head on her crossed arms.

'Izzy's with me,' Alex says quietly and Tash looks up. She looks directly at him, her puffy eyes narrowing, and then looks to the side of him, right at me.

'Where?'

'I'm here,' I whisper. I reach out across the table and put my fingers on the back of her hand.

'Oh,' she says, grabbing my hand with both of hers and squeezing it a bit too tightly. 'Oh, thank fuck.'

'Do you want to get out of here?' I ask her.

'I…' She frowns, looking confused. 'I ordered food.'

'You ordered food?'

'I feel…' She sits back and puts one hand on her stomach. 'I feel like there's a hole. Here. I wanted…' She looks confused again. 'Soup.'

'Soup.'

She nods.

'That makes sense,' Alex says. 'Comfort food.'

Tash nods. 'My mum always made me soup. When I was sad.'

Her voice is tiny and I can't bear it. Not Tash. I stand up and move around the table to sit down next to her on her side of the booth.

'Budge up,' I say, my mouth next to her ear. I wrap my arms round her, she presses her face against my neck and I feel her tears running down inside the collar of my t-shirt.

I turn my body to shelter her from the rest of the pub, but then I realise I'm not sheltering her at all. I can't.

'Does this look—' I start to ask Alex, but right then the waiter arrives with Tash's food: a bowl of what looks like tomato soup and a plate with half a baguette and a pot of butter.

'I'll just get your cutlery,' the waiter says, looking down at the table and clearly trying really hard not to look at Tash.

I stroke her hair as she sniffles against my neck. 'I can't believe it,' I hear her mumble. 'What did I do wrong?'

'Nothing,' I say into the top of her head. 'You didn't do anything wrong. It'll be okay. Eat your soup and then come back to mine and it'll all be okay.'

At least, I hope it will.

*

'Do we need to go and collect anything from your flat?' Alex asks Tash as we get into the taxi about half an hour later.

Tash just shakes her head at Alex, and pulls at my hand so I'm sitting down next to her. She curls into me the same way she did in the pub. I'm not sure I've ever seen her like this before. When she split up with her boyfriend before we moved to London, she didn't cry at all. She got absolutely hammered, threw all the photos of the two of them into a bin outside McDonald's and told me never to mention him again.

Alex is sitting opposite on the drop-down seat and looking between me and Tash. He looks concerned and it makes me want to kiss him. I know I should be thinking about my best friend and her heartbreak – and I am – but Alex has been so gentle with Tash that it makes me want to tie him to a bed. That's probably weird. I need to ask Tash about that. But maybe not right now.

'Have you got wine?' Tash asks me as soon as we're inside my flat.

Alex paid for the taxi again; I need to remember to pay him back. The thought of money makes anxiety prickle in my belly, but I can deal with that another day. I need to deal with Tash today.

'Yes, don't worry,' I tell her, tugging her jacket off her shoulders and hanging it over the back of a chair.

'Not now, though,' she says, her head slumping forward. 'Can I just sleep?'

'Of course. Do you—'

I don't get to finish my question because Tash just heads into my bedroom, without looking back.

'Do you think she needs anything?' I ask Alex.

'I think she just needs to sleep,' Alex says. He walks right up to me and puts one hand on my left shoulder. His other hand slides up my right arm before finding my other shoulder and then he pulls me against his chest.

'You're really good at that,' I tell him. 'Knowing where I am, I mean.'

I feel him laugh into the top of my hair. 'I know. It's weird. If I close my eyes, I can't even tell you're invisible.'

My breath catches in my chest and I make myself breathe out slowly and carefully.

'You were good with Tash, too,' I say as soon as I can.

He hums. 'Well, you know, I've been there.'

'Oh yeah,' I say. His chin is resting on the top of my head and I like it. I feel grounded.

'How about you?' he says. 'Ever had your heart broken?'

I shake my head, feeling his chin drag across my hair.

'No?' he says.

'No.'

'Why not?'

'I...' I frown. 'I'm not sure. I think... I protect myself too well.'

He laughs. 'Yeah?'

'Yeah. I... There was one boyfriend when I was eighteen. And I really... We both... I think... Shit, sorry, I can't finish a sentence.'

'It's okay. You don't have to tell me if—'

'No, I want to. But I haven't thought about it for a while and I'm just not sure...'

'Should we sit down?' Alex squeezes and releases me, sliding his hand down my arm and into my hand. He leads me over to the sofa and I sit down in what was always Max's spot, but which I have now reclaimed with cushions and a blanket. I lean back against the arm of the sofa, tucking my feet up under me.

'So,' I say. 'His name was Danny.'

'Wait,' Alex says. 'Don't tell me. You had a summer romance and you thought you'd never see him again, but then it turned out you were both at the same high school—'

I throw a cushion at him and it hits him square in the face. He drops it down onto his lap and grins at me. 'Sorry, couldn't resist.'

'No. We met in the square we used to hang out at after school.'

'The square?'

'Yeah, just like... a square. In front of some shops.'

'What did you do there?'

'Just... hung out, really. There wasn't anything to do.'

'Okay,' Alex says. 'Just trying to picture the scene.'

'So, yeah, we met at the square. And we started going out. And I really liked him. And he really liked me. I think. I mean, he said he did.'

'Right. Sounds good.'

'It was, yeah. For a while. But I was always sort of... I never really believed that he liked me as much as he said he did. I thought he was joking or exaggerating or that he'd maybe convinced himself he liked me, but he didn't really. I thought for a while that maybe he was only going out with me to get to Tash.'

Alex is shaking his head, his brows pulled together in a frown.

'Yeah,' I say. 'I know. Self-esteem issues. This isn't news. But then I had to go to university. He wanted us to keep going out, like long distance. He said that he loved me. And I... I thought I loved him. But when he said it, I can remember thinking that it was just ridiculous. That of course he didn't love me. Of course I didn't love him. We were just kids.'

'You were eighteen?'

'Almost nineteen by then. Yeah. Old enough to know.'

'Yeah,' Alex says.

'It just seemed unimaginable to me,' I say. 'I don't get it now. I really don't. I liked him. Maybe I loved him. But I couldn't leave someone I loved, so instead I pretended I didn't. And I pretended so well that I believed myself. How fucked up is that?'

'It's not fucked up,' he says quietly. 'You were protecting yourself. Like you said.'

I stare at him. His gingery hair. His stubble. The way one of his eyebrows is sort of tufty at the end. If I'd met him in a bar,

I'm not sure I'd have looked at him twice. But here, on my sofa…
I like his face.

'Have you fallen asleep?' he says.

I laugh. 'Sorry, no. Just thinking.'

''Cos you know you've got an unfair advantage with this invisibility thing.'

'I won't abuse it, I promise,' I say.

And then my head fills with an image of me unbuttoning Alex's shirt, undoing his belt, sliding my hands across his shoulders and down his stomach while he tries to touch me but can't because he can't see me. I cross my legs, squeezing my thighs together.

Alex reaches over and I watch his fingers as he touches my knee. I close my eyes so I can feel them without the weirdness of seeing them hovering there on what looks like nothing.

I feel him moving closer. I can smell the clean soapy scent of his skin. Or maybe it's his hair. His other hand is on my other knee.

'Is this okay?' he says and his voice is closer.

'Yeah.' I lean forward to kiss him, but hit him in the face with my forehead.

'Shit!' he says, dropping against the back of the sofa.

'Sorry,' I say, leaning forward again and sliding one hand over his cheek. There's a red mark blooming on his forehead. 'Sorry, I had my eyes closed.'

He laughs. 'I think maybe it's a good idea for one of us to actually see.'

'No, you're right,' I say. 'I'm sorry.' I move closer so that I'm kneeling up next to him and move my other hand up to his face.

'Is this okay?' I ask him.

He smiles. 'You're not going to head-butt me again?'

'I'm going to try hard not to.'

He tips his face up and I press my mouth down on his, his arms immediately sliding around my back and pulling me more firmly against him. My eyes are open, but his are closed, his long eyelashes casting shadows on his cheeks.

'Hey,' Tash says from behind me. 'I can't sleep. My brain won't shut up. God, I feel like shit.'

I pull away from Alex, feeling instantly colder when I'm not leaning against him, and turn to look back at Tash.

She's tied her hair up in a loose bun and she looks tired and drained.

'Come and sit down,' I tell her. I can't even look at Alex, but he instantly moves up to the other end of the sofa and directs Tash to the part he'd been sitting on – we'd both been sitting on – until a few seconds ago.

'Thanks,' Tash says, sitting. She rubs both hands over her face and stretches, rolling her neck from side to side. 'And thanks for coming to get me,' she says, pushing her shoulders back and groaning at the stretch. 'I… God. Today has been total dog shit.'

'What happened?' I ask.

'I'm going to go and get some wine,' Alex says, standing up. 'And… a takeaway? Do you need anything?'

My stomach rumbles right on cue and I realise that I haven't eaten. I was planning to get some food when Tash phoned and then I thought about ordering something at the pub, but there's the whole 'eating while invisible' issue.

'Could you get some chips maybe?' I ask him.

'I'll get fish and chips,' he says. 'Tash? You hungry?'

'I could eat some chips,' she says. 'Let me give you some money.'

'No,' Alex says. 'Don't worry about it.'

I start to stand up. 'Honestly. I need to. You paid for the cabs and—'

'It's fine,' he says. 'You two talk. I'll get food. And more wine, right?'

'Yeah,' I say, looking at Tash. 'Please.'

Alex leaves and I rest my socked feet on Tash's thigh.

'Hey,' I say.

She reaches down and wraps her hand around my ankle. 'Fucking hell, Izzy. What am I going to do?'

'You're going to stay here until you feel better,' I tell her. 'Right?' She nods.

'Do you want to talk about it?' I ask.

We sit in silence for a few seconds and then she says, 'He's fallen in love with someone else. Rob.'

'Oh Tash,' I say, reaching out and picking up her hand.

'I thought he was in love with me. He said that he was in love with me. And then he comes back from America and tells me that he's never been in love with me. He thought he was, but then he met someone else and was like… oh! This is how it should feel.'

'Fuck,' I say.

Tash laughs. 'I know. And I feel… I feel like such a fucking idiot. All this time, I've felt so… We had a good thing, you know? I got to have this man at home. This man who loved me and it was comfortable and secure and I still got to go and fuck other people. I thought it was perfect. I thought I was so fucking clever.'

'It's not you,' I tell her, stroking the back of her hand with my thumb.

'It is, though,' she says forcefully. 'It is! I sat there with you in that bar, telling you how it was down to you that you'd settled for Max, that you could do better, that you were scared and all the time I was—'

She starts to cry again, huge gulping sobs, and I crawl across the sofa and wrap my arms around her.

'You know you asked if I was punishing him. Rob. When I didn't go to Texas?'

'I remember,' I say.

'He was with her,' she says. 'I didn't know for sure. But I suspected. I didn't go because he didn't ask me. Because he knew she was going to be there and he wanted to be with her.'

'Oh Tash,' I say. 'I'm so sorry.'

She shakes her head. 'It's fine. He…' She screws her face up and I reach over and hold her hand. 'At least he was honest with me, you know? I just wish… I wish I'd been more honest with him.'

'It's okay, you know,' I say. 'That you only knew when it was too late. I mean… I don't mean it's okay. I mean, you can't help that. You didn't do it on purpose.'

She turns to look in my direction and she's already shaking her head. 'That's the stupid thing. I'm not in love with him either. But I thought it was enough. I thought it was enough for both of us. But now he's like "oh no, this is so much better" and I think… so what about me? Why don't I want better? Why was it enough for me?'

'You don't… I mean, it's not essential for you to fall in love, you know. It's okay for you to want what you want.'

'But it's bullshit,' she says vehemently. 'Both of us – me and you – trying to protect ourselves. You moving in with someone you didn't even like.'

I almost argue automatically, but she's right.

'And me fooling myself all this time. But we both got hurt anyway.' She turns towards me, pulling her legs up underneath her, and reaches out her hands. I take them both.

'We should make a vow,' she says.

'Oh god.'

She laughs. 'No, not like when we were teenagers. A real one. We should make a vow to always be honest. With ourselves. With each other. With whoever we're seeing. If we like someone we should tell them. And if we don't like someone – or if they're shit in bed – we should stop seeing them, no arguments, no excuses. What do you say?'

'Of course,' I say, squeezing her hands. 'I promise.'

I want to ask her about Liam. But I know Tash. If she wanted to talk about Liam, she'd be talking about Liam.

'If I close my eyes,' she says after a while, her voice croaky, 'I can't even tell you're invisible.'

'I know,' I say. 'That's what Alex said.'

'He's really good,' she mumbles. 'You should get that locked down.'

I laugh. 'I think it's a bit early for that.'

'Also you should never listen to me again. About anything. I talk shit.'

'You don't,' I say, stroking her hair back from her forehead. 'You're very wise.'

'What am I going to do, Iz?'

'You're going to be fine,' I say and kiss her temple.

'Can I really stay here? Rob's selling the flat. They're getting a place together. He—' She starts to cry again and I hold her tighter, resting my cheek on the top of her head.

'Of course you can stay,' I say. 'It'll be like old times. If we listen really carefully, maybe we'll hear someone wanking upstairs.'

Alex comes back with wine, milk and bread, along with the fish and chips. He gets plates from the cupboard, sets the table in the kitchen and puts the kettle on for tea. I turn to watch him over the back of the sofa, fascinated. I don't remember Max ever setting the table. We ate at the table when he first moved in with me, but it wasn't long before he was eating on his lap in front of the TV. For a while, I sat at the table by myself, but it made me sad, so I ended up eating on my lap too.

'Ready?' Alex says, raising his eyebrows at me.

'I'm going to go and wash my face,' Tash says, uncurling herself from the sofa and squeezing my hand before letting go and heading towards the bathroom.

'Thank you for this,' I tell Alex as I stand up. My leg is aching from the way I've been sitting and I rub at it, feeling my thigh muscle cramp and release.

'No worries,' Alex says. 'Where are you?'

I'm leaning against the back of the sofa and looking at him. He's so relaxed and confident and comfortable in himself. I like it.

'I like you,' I tell him. 'You're nice.'

His eyes widen and his face splits into a huge smile as he takes a couple of steps towards me. I stand up all the way, reach my hands out and flatten them against his chest.

'I like you too,' he says, his hands smoothing over my shoulders and down my arms.

I take another step and rest the top of my head against his collarbone. I can feel his breath moving my hair.

'We should go on a date,' Alex says. 'Once you're, you know, back to yourself.'

I laugh. 'Yeah. Back to myself.' But I feel more like myself now than I ever have before.

'That looks weird,' Tash says, walking back into the kitchen. 'You standing there, holding nothing.'

'I'm not holding nothing,' Alex says. 'I'm holding Izzy.'

I look over at Tash and she's smiling right at me. 'Yeah,' she says. 'You are.'

CHAPTER FIFTEEN

'Do you ever feel like you took a wrong turn somewhere and you're not sure you can get back on the right road?' Tash asks as she dishes out the fish and chips.

'No, never,' Alex says, his face serious.

'Really?' I say, picking a chip off my plate. 'God.'

'Sorry,' Alex says. 'That's a lie. I feel like that almost all the time.'

Tash snorts and Alex smiles. 'Not so much lately, if I'm honest. Things are mostly pretty good. But I've felt like that for a lot of my life.'

'And so… what do you do about it?' Tash says.

'Have you ever used GPS in a car?' Alex asks us.

I shake my head. 'I can't drive.'

'I've used it on my phone,' Tash says.

'Ah right. So they give you directions, right? But if you go wrong, they just work out a different route. And while they do it, the little electronic voice tells you it's doing it. It says something like "recalibrating" or "finding alternative route".'

'Huh,' I say.

'So I need to recalibrate,' Tash says.

'Yup,' Alex says. 'Or find an alternative route.'

'That is actually really helpful,' Tash tells him.

'Yeah?' he says, his face breaking into a grin. 'I was just thinking maybe it was bollocks.'

I laugh. 'No. Definitely not bollocks.'

I look from Alex to Tash and back again. They like each other. And that's a good thing. And I'm not worried about it. I once asked Max if he fancied Tash (I like to torture myself, I guess) and he said she was out of his league. Which made me feel great. But with Alex, I get that he likes her, but I don't feel like he's seeing me as second division, or whatever. That feels like something for me to recalibrate.

I'm not sure there's anything more delicious than fish and chips, particularly when you're hungry. I make a chip butty with so much butter that it melts and runs down my arms.

'Iz. I can see your hands,' Tash says, after a minute.

I hold my hands up and rub them together, smearing butter over them both. My hands appear in front of me, sort of blurry and vague, like an undeveloped photo.

'What's that?' Alex asks.

'Butter.'

He opens and closes his mouth, one of his hands reaching out towards mine.

'Don't even think about it,' Tash says. 'I've got a broken heart and I'm not sitting here stuffing my face with chips while you develop some sort of butter kink.'

'Oh my god!' I snort. 'That's not—'

But then I see Alex's face and he looks like he wants to eat me. I stare at his mouth and I want to wish Tash away and let Alex lick the butter off my fingers.

'Shit,' I say quietly.

'Seriously,' Tash says. 'Knock it the fuck off. I'm really happy for you both, but not today, Satan.'

Alex laughs and picks up his tea, draining it to the bottom of the mug. 'More wine?' he asks, faux-brightly.

I laugh. 'Please.'

*

'Call me if you need me,' Alex says when we've finished the fish and chips and the wine and he needs to get home and sleep before work tomorrow.

'I'm getting a strong feeling of déjà vu here,' I say.

Alex grins. 'That's all we need.'

'Thanks for today,' Tash says, tipping her head back on the sofa to look at him upside down.

'No worries,' he says. 'You take care of yourself.'

I follow him through the kitchen to the door and he stops and reaches out to me again. I love it. I love the way his hands on me make me feel. I just want to lean against him and let him hold me. I would totally let him shove his hand down my jeans at a bus stop.

'Thank you,' I say again.

'You don't have to keep thanking me. It was no big deal.' His fingers walk up my spine.

'It was,' I say. 'It was to me and it was to Tash.'

He tips his head and I press my forehead against his.

'Well,' he says. 'Then you're welcome.'

'I don't want to kiss,' I say, my mouth almost touching his. 'I mean, I do. But not now. Here. With Tash over there. I want it to be…' I shake my head. 'Can we do it another time?'

'Fuck,' he says and I feel his breath against my lips. 'I really need to get home and, you know, sort myself out.'

I laugh. 'Oh my god.'

'And,' he says quietly, his mouth next to my ear. 'We're totally investigating that butter thing at some point.'

CHAPTER SIXTEEN

'I had an idea,' Tash says in the morning.

We're sitting on the sofa, TV turned to *This Morning* but with the sound down, and Tash is eating what I think might be her sixth piece of toast. Not that I'm judging.

'Oh god,' I say.

'No,' she says, wiping butter off her chin with the back of her hand. 'It's a good one.'

'Go on…'

'You're invisible, right?' she says.

I just stare at her. Not that she can tell.

'Well, that gives you an advantage for the pitch,' she says. She puts the crust of the current piece of toast back on the plate and picks up a fresh piece.

'Er, how does it?' I ask.

I've already had three pieces of toast too, but seeing Tash merrily crunching away makes me reach for another.

'You can go and do a recce,' she says, a few crumbs flying out of her mouth.

'Where?'

'Fancy Bantams,' she says. 'Duh.'

'Don't "duh" me,' I say. 'How am I supposed to do that?'

'We get a cab there. I wait for you somewhere nearby – I'm sure there'll be a Starbucks or something – and you go in and have a look around. Earwig on the staff. Rummage through their unmentionables. I dunno. Use your imagination.'

'Hmm,' I say as I chew my toast. 'Hmm.'

'And do not talk to me about ethics,' Tash says, reaching over and picking up the remote as Joe Wicks appears on screen to do the cooking segment. 'Fuck ethics. You're invisible. You're already at a disadvantage. You might as well use it any way you can.'

'Hmm,' I say again. I'm not completely convinced, but I'm willing to think about it.

'No time like the present,' Tash is saying half an hour later, once she's finished drooling over Joe Wicks making a turkey burger and eaten all the toast.

I sigh. 'I suppose.'

'Come on,' she says. 'I'm devastated and heartbroken. I need to be entertained.'

She says it lightly, but her voice cracks a bit and the thing is, she is devastated and heartbroken, I know she is. And I do want to take care of her. And I also do need to get on with writing the pitch. I hate it when she's right.

'I'll get dressed,' I say.

'That's my girl,' she says. She tries to slap my arse, but misses completely.

The Fancy Bantams office isn't actually that far away. It's on an industrial estate just outside East Finchley. There's no Starbucks, but there's a huge Tesco about five minutes' walk away, so Tash goes there and I tell her I'll come and find her in about an hour.

The main door is electric, so I walk in without any problem and wait in the reception area until a man comes in and greets the receptionist before opening the door to the Fancy Bantams office with a swipe card. I walk right up close behind him and manage to follow him inside before the door closes.

The office is open plan and huge, with metal staircases and a mezzanine floor. There are enormous windows at the top, but hardly any windows at all at the bottom. All around the walls are lit-up signs with inspirational slogans like 'Do what you love, love what you do', 'Be awesome' and 'Rock it!'

I've seen photos of their old office in one of the files and it was nothing like this. It was staid and boring and practical.

I can hear music playing, but it's fairly low. Other than that the only sound I can hear is the sound of fingers tapping on keyboards and mobile alerts. It's fairly similar to our office, really, just on a much bigger and more hipster scale.

I walk over to the closest desk where a man is leaning too far back on his chair and talking into his mobile.

'We're literally ripping up the rule book,' he says and I roll my eyes and walk further into the office.

At the far end there's a row of tables with booth seating like you'd find in a diner. Most of them are empty, but there are four young-looking women sitting around one of them and I head over and lean against the next table. They're not talking; all four of them are leaning over a huge piece of paper on the table. I can't see whether they're writing or drawing or doing a crossword, so I move round and stand at the end of their table. My stomach rolls with nerves – it's hard to believe they can possibly not be aware of me, standing right next to them, but of course they're not. And then I feel guilty for spying.

'*Fuck ethics!*' I hear Tash say and so I lean forward as far as I can without risking bumping the table and then one of the women says, 'Urban camouflage?'

The other three all sit up straight and stare at her.

'That works,' one of them says. She's white but with dread-locks down to her waist. She doesn't seem to be wearing any make-up apart from blue lipstick. Not very camouflaged, urban or otherwise.

I take a couple of steps back and look at all four of the women. None of them appear to be wearing Fancy Bantams clothes. And now that I think about it, the guy at the first desk wasn't either. Everyone's wearing much more interesting stuff.

At the end of the row of tables, there's an empty office. It's all glass and it doesn't have a door, so I walk straight in and look around. There's a triangular desk in one corner and then diagonally opposite there's a huge black box. I walk over and peer at it. It looks like a ballot box, like when you go to vote. They're actually going to have the staff write their agency preference and put it in a ballot box? It seems really unlikely that they're even considering staying with Houghton & Peel. Pitching at all might well be a complete waste of time.

I'm looking at a framed certificate hanging on the side of a bookcase when someone walks in. As usual, a feeling of panic floods over me before I realise it's fine, I can't be seen. It's another young-ish looking guy. He's pretty good-looking, even though he's wearing a beanie indoors. He sits down behind the desk, fiddles with his mobile and then says, 'Hey. Calvin, hi.'

He swings away from me on his chair and I head back out to the main part of the office.

I spend the rest of my allotted hour just wandering around, listening to any conversations I come across, reading bits of promotional material and stuff stuck on the pinboard, looking at framed photos on the walls. I have to wait by the door for a few minutes before someone leaves and I can follow them out, but then I make my way over to Tesco and find Tash sitting next to the trolley lockers, a massive mug of tea from the cafe clutched between her hands and an utterly dejected look on her face.

I sit down next to her and put my arm around her and she jumps out of her skin, knocking the table with her knees and splashing tea everywhere.

'Sorry,' I whisper.

'Jesus fucking Christ,' she says.

I hear someone nearby tut and Tash rolls her eyes.

'You should wear a bell or something,' Tash says, not even caring that as far as anyone else is concerned, she's talking to herself in a Tesco. 'God, I swear you forget you're invisible sometimes.'

She's right. I do.

'Don't be mean,' I say into her ear. 'Are you okay? You looked miserable when I came in.'

She takes her phone out and holds it up to her ear – Alex's trick. 'I am miserable.'

'I'm sorry,' I say and squeeze her.

'S'okay. My own fault. How did it go?'

'It was okay,' I say. 'Can't really talk here.'

She drains the last of her tea – most of it is pooled on the table – and stands up. 'Let's get out of here then.'

'Urban camouflage?' Tash says, once we're back at my flat and sitting at opposite ends of the sofa. 'Ugh.'

'I know,' I say.

'So they want to blend in,' Tash says. 'That's the point. I mean, you say "urban camouflage" and I immediately think of a grey bloke against a grey building, you know?'

On the Fancy Bantams website, there is literally a photo of a man all in grey, leaning against a grey wall. The only colour in the photo is a bright yellow flower growing out from between the bricks.

I nod. 'Yes. But they want to blend in in an edgy way. Apparently. And I need to come up with something fast,' I say. 'Or it's going to be too late. Although if I'm still invisible I'm fucked anyway.'

'Not necessarily,' Tash says. 'We could make a video or something. You could do a voiceover. Don't give up. I'm sure Alex would help. We'll find a way round it.'

I really hope so. As much as I'm nervous about the pitch, I want to be able to do it. I want to rise to the challenge. And I want the promotion. I think.

CHAPTER SEVENTEEN

'Urban camouflage?' Alex says. 'God.'

'I know.'

I take Max's favourite mug out of the cupboard and drop it into the kitchen bin. There's stuff of Max's all over this flat and I'm chucking it out as soon as I find it.

'I don't think I even know what that means,' Alex says.

'Damn,' I say, putting my phone on speaker so I can pull the washing out of the machine. 'I was hoping you might have some brilliant insights.'

He laughs. 'Sorry. I'll definitely think on it, though.'

'I mean, it's just the future of the company and basically my entire life that's at stake,' I say.

'No pressure then.'

'Nope. I've been thinking about that quote, "Why blend in when you were born to stand out?" You know? But that's the thing, isn't it? People want to stand out – they want to be seen – but not too much.'

'Right,' Alex says.

'I think we all want to feel like we're being seen,' I say. 'Without actually drawing too much attention to ourselves. Does that make sense?'

'It does,' Alex says. 'It makes a lot of sense.'

'Good,' I say. ''Cos that's all I've got so far.'

Alex laughs. 'How's Tash?'

'She's not too bad,' I say. 'We're watching *Thelma & Louise* tonight. It's the perfect post break-up film.'

'Yeah?' he says. 'What's it about?'

I shut the washing machine door and pick up my phone, leaning back against the countertop. 'What? You don't know *Thelma & Louise*?'

'I don't think so,' he says. 'Is it new? Who's in it?'

'No, it's not new! It's from, like, the nineties. Geena Davis and Susan Sarandon. It's a classic!'

'I promise I'll watch it next time it's on.'

'No,' I say.

'No?'

I cross the kitchen and open the bedroom door. 'You should come and watch it tonight. With us?'

Tash is sitting up against my headboard, one leg crossed over the other, painting her toenails.

'It's all right if Alex comes to watch it too, right?' I ask her, holding the phone against my shoulder.

She jumps, dropping the nail varnish on my duvet. 'Shit! Sorry! You scared me. Tell him to bring that bell.'

'Don't worry about that duvet,' I tell her. 'I never liked it anyway. So? Alex? He's never seen *Thelma & Louise*.'

'He's fucking what?!' Tash says, screwing the top back onto the nail varnish and standing up, her toes curled up so they're not touching the carpet. 'Yeah. Tell him to bring wine.'

'We've got wine,' I say. 'And, honestly, put the duvet cover in the bin.'

Tash hobbles to the bottom of the bed and starts unpopping the poppers. 'We could always use more wine,' she says.

'What do you think?' I say into the phone.

'I'm wondering what's going on over there,' he says and I can hear him smiling.

'All good clean fun!' I say.

'Shame,' he says and butterflies flicker in my belly.

I want to say something sexy and flirty like, *Well you're not here yet, are you?* But instead I say, 'Tash says can you bring wine?'

'I haven't said I'm coming yet,' he says.

I want to say something sexy and flirty to that too, but nope.

'But you are, though, aren't you?'

'I'll be there in an hour,' he says.

'Oh, this film!' Alex says, not long after the opening titles.

'Have you seen it?' I ask him.

He's sitting at one end of the sofa and Tash is at the other. I'm in the middle with my feet up on the coffee table, a cushion on my lap so they know vaguely where I am.

He shakes his head. 'No. But I recognise it from "best of" compilations, that kind of thing. Brad Pitt's in it, right?'

'Yeah he is!' Tash says, sounding like Joey from *Friends*. 'He's never been hotter.'

We're mostly quiet during the rest of the film, apart from yelling, cheering the two women on, covering our eyes at the more tense parts.

'I'd love to do this,' Alex says as we watch them drive through tall red rocks, dust flying up behind their convertible.

'What? Run from the law?' Tash says.

Alex laughs. 'US road trip.'

'That's what I was saving up for,' I say. 'Well, sort of.'

'How sort of?' Alex asks.

'It was more kind of a security fund. But I thought that if I got to ten grand, I'd take some out and do a US road trip.'

'Ten grand?' Alex says, turning slightly towards me. 'How much did you have saved?'

'Seven and a half,' I tell him. 'It was from an inheritance. Mostly.'

'Wow,' Alex says. 'I can't imagine having that much saved.'

'I know, right?' Tash says. She's pulled her legs up so she's sitting cross-legged and leaning back against the end of the sofa, half-turned between us and the TV. 'Izzy likes security.'

'Everyone likes security,' I say. 'Don't they?'

'I think... maybe,' Alex says. 'But there's something to be said for freedom too. Being able to just take off whenever you want.'

I frown. I don't want Alex to take off. I want him to stay.

'You're like me,' Tash tells him. 'I don't like responsibility.'

'But sometimes you need to be responsible,' I say. 'I mean, if I wasn't responsible, where would you be living now?' I mean it to sound light and teasing, but it doesn't come out quite right.

'Ouch,' Tash says, leaning forward to pick up her wine from the coffee table.

'Sorry,' I say. 'I didn't mean—'

'No,' Tash says. 'You're right. You just, you know, sounded like your mother.'

I look at her and see the small smile she's hiding behind her glass.

'You can fuck right off,' I say, laughing.

I'm already crying before the ending of the film. I've seen it so many times and I cry every time. And I also think that maybe, somehow, they'll be okay. Last time we watched it, Tash and I said we were going to turn it off before the very end and pretend that Thelma and Louise somehow evaded all the cops and made it to Mexico and are still living there now, relaxed and happy and together.

But I can't do it. I need to watch it right to the end.

'Oh shit,' Alex says, and when I turn to look at him, he's leaning forward, elbows on his knees, his face tense. 'They're not—' he says.

I sniffle and he turns to look at me, reaching one hand out across the sofa. I slide my fingers between his and squeeze his hand.

'Oh shit,' he says again, looking back at the screen.

Thelma's revving the engine and Harvey Keitel's running and the dust is flying and I can hear Tash sniffing too.

As the final shot freezes on the screen, Alex says, 'Holy shit,' and I rub my wet face with my free hand.

'I fucking love that film,' Tash says, her voice thick with tears. And then, 'Hey! Iz, I can see you!'

'What?' I say, but I realise instantly. The tears. My face is wet.

I look at Alex and he's looking back at me with the most incredible expression on his face. Like he can't believe he can see me. Can't believe I'm real. He leans towards me, tugging on my hand at the same time and Tash says, 'So I'm going to go and have a shower.' The sofa shifts as she stands up, but I don't turn around; I'm staring at Alex.

'A really long, loud, shower,' Tash says. Her voice is further away, she must be crossing the kitchen. 'Do you understand what I'm saying?'

'Yes,' I say, but it comes out as a whisper.

Alex gives Tash a thumbs-up, but he's still looking at me. His eyes move down to my lips and I feel my breath catch in my chest.

He reaches his hand out towards my face. I catch it and guide it to my cheek.

'Izzy,' he says. 'You look…'

His thumb strokes my cheekbone and his fingers walk down to my jaw. I shiver as his thumb brushes across my chin and then moves up and glides across my bottom lip. Without even thinking, I touch it with my tongue and Alex groans.

I run my fingers along his jaw and he closes his eyes. I lean towards him and kiss the side of his neck. He moans softly right next to my ear. His hand moves up my back, his fingers grazing the back of my neck, and then his hand is in my hair, holding the back of my head. Closing my eyes, I press my mouth to his. His fingers tighten in my hair and I brace myself so I'm not tempted to press my entire body against him. But I want to. I really want to. Alex's other hand slides down my side and round to my lower back, pulling me to him. I hear myself sigh as I let go and fall against him.

His mouth opens wider, his tongue sliding against mine. I can feel his erection against my thigh and that's what makes me stop.

'I can't do this,' I murmur against his mouth.

'Oh go on,' he says and I laugh.

'It's not that I don't want to,' I say. It takes all my strength to push myself back from him, to peel my body off his. 'I really do.'

'Don't stop then,' Alex says, pulling me towards him again.

'I want to do it,' I say. 'I do. But not like this. Not while I'm... you know.'

'I can feel you,' he says. 'When I close my eyes, I can't even tell you're invisible.'

'But I can,' I say. 'If we do this, I want you to see me.'

I shuffle back on the sofa so we're no longer touching at all.

'I need more wine,' I say.

'I want to see you too,' Alex says. 'But is it okay to say that was... really good?'

I laugh. 'Yeah. It was. I just don't... I don't want this to be a kinky thing.'

Alex grins and I can't help grinning back. 'You're worried I'm an invisibility perv?'

'No! I mean, yeah, a bit. But not really. 'Cos that's not a thing. Obviously. I just...'

'It's okay,' he says. 'I get it.'

'Really?'

'Really.' He smiles. 'This is a... unique situation and you don't know how to deal with it.'

'Yeah,' I say.

I stare at him and he's looking back at me, but he can't see me. Except I feel like he can. How can that be? And how did I never notice how sexy he is? He's beautiful. I want to kiss him again.

'Fuck it,' I say. I lean forward, bracing my hands on his chest, and press my mouth to his. He makes a surprised little sound, then I lick over his tongue and he groans.

'You're so—' he says, but I press hard up against him, pushing him back against the arm of the sofa.

'So good—' he says, surging forward and pushing his hands into my hair, his thumbs brushing over my cheekbones.

'Good to—'

I dip my head and lick his neck just under his ear and he pushes back against me until I'm tipping back on the sofa.

'See you,' he finishes as he leans over me. He brushes his thumb over my eyebrow and I close my eyes.

I slide my hand under the back of his t-shirt. His skin is warm and I fit my fingers between the knots of his spine. I'm suddenly aware that I can hear the shower running and I smile.

'She's really showering,' Alex says, leaning down to press his lips to my collarbone.

'She's probably not,' I say. 'She's probably sitting on the loo and scrolling through Tinder.'

Alex laughs and I feel it thrum over my skin. He moves back up to my face, kissing up my jaw, one hand in my hair again, the other braced against the sofa, holding him up over me.

'Can you still see me?' I whisper, even though I know he can't.

'I can if I close my eyes,' he says. 'You're beautiful.'

I tip my head up and open my mouth against his, licking against his lips, using the flat of my hand to press him down against me. He moves his arm up over my head and lowers himself on top of me.

'Is this okay?' he says into my neck.

I tip my hips up, rubbing myself against him. 'Yes. More.'

He groans again and shifts against me. I arch my back.

'Oh god. Yeah. There.'

'Yeah?' he says, his hips moving.

I can't speak. I open my eyes and look down at the top of his head as he pushes my top up and kisses across my chest. I love his hair. I love the colour of it and the way it feels under my fingers. I tug at the short hairs at the back of his neck and then gather his hair into a ponytail in my hand. He groans again as I pull at it lightly.

'Want me to stop?' he says, his mouth against my skin.

'Don't you fucking dare,' I say and he laughs.

His tongue swirls around my nipple and my hips curl up again as I tip my head back.

'Yeah?' he says again.

'Please.'

He starts to suck and I pull my legs up around his waist, shifting my hips until I can feel his erection pressing right between my legs.

I hear a sound and for a second I'm worried it's Tash coming back, but then I realise it's me. I squeeze my eyes closed and focus on Alex's mouth and hips and dick. My hands are moving on his back, pressing him into me as I try to lift myself up to meet him. There's a wet sound as he moves from one breast to the other and I feel the cool air on my wet nipple.

'Fuck,' Alex says, his voice low and rough. 'I can see you… where I've been licking. I can see…'

He doesn't get to finish because the idea of it pushes me over the edge and I come, squeezing him between my legs as he presses his face into my neck.

CHAPTER EIGHTEEN

'So clearly the sex is better with Alex,' Tash says, later.

Alex left, after we spent a ridiculously long amount of time kissing goodbye at the door, and now Tash and I are sitting up in bed, scrolling our phones.

'You weren't meant to be listening!' I say, kicking her under the duvet.

'I wasn't listening,' she says. 'But I still heard. Noisy bastards.'

'Ugh,' I say. 'You're the worst.'

'I left you alone, didn't I? I could see he was all…' She waggles her eyebrows at me, sticks out her tongue.

'Ugh,' I say again.

'He really likes you, I think,' she says.

I smile. 'I really like him.'

'And the sex…?'

'God, Tash,' I say. 'The sex is… it was never like that with Max. I had no fucking idea. I can't believe it. All these years. Now I see why you're—'

'Such a slut?' she says, grinning.

'So into it, is what I was going to say.'

'Yeah,' she says. 'That's the thing with sex. When it's good it's really good. But when it's bad, it's the fucking worst.'

'I didn't know it was bad with Max, though,' I say, putting my phone down on my lap. 'I just thought that's what sex was like. I couldn't understand what the fuss was about.'

'But you slept with people before Max, though,' Tash says, putting her phone down too and turning towards me.

'Yeah,' I say. 'But only a couple. And it wasn't great with them either. I mean, it wasn't bad, but it was only okay.'

'And with Alex?'

I shake my head. 'It's just… With Max it was sort of like something he did to me, you know? And I really mostly did it because he wanted it. But with Alex, it was both of us. And I didn't even really have to think about it.'

'That's good,' Tash says. 'That's how it should be, I think.'

'And I think…' I say. 'I think that's to do with being invisible too. You know, with Max sometimes I'd worry about how I looked. To him. I'd hold my belly in or I'd avoid certain positions 'cos I didn't want him to see me like that. But now…'

'Yeah,' Tash says. 'I get how that would help.'

'I just don't think about it. It means I can think about me more. I mean… I think about Alex too, of course, but with Max I never felt like I was really there. I was thinking of… someone else. Or something else. Work, sometimes.'

'This is good, then. I said that, didn't I? I said it could be good for you.'

'You did,' I say, nodding. 'How weird, though. And the weirdest thing is that I never really worried about it. Or even thought about it. I just kind of accepted that that was how it should be.'

'That's not your fault, though,' Tash says. 'The male fucking gaze. Everywhere. We almost always see sex from the man's perspective, I don't think it's a big surprise that we do that ourselves.'

'No,' I say. 'But god. How shit is that?'

'Right?' Tash says. 'But talking about sex from a man's perspective, how tempted was I to come out and peek at Alex humping the air?'

'Oh my god,' I say, covering my face even though she can't see it. 'You didn't!'

'Course I didn't!' She laughs. 'But I wanted to. I bet it looks hilarious.'

'You're not helping. And also we weren't having sex.'

'No? It sounded like it.'

'I mean… I guess it depends what you call sex? But we didn't, you know.'

'You both came,' Tash says. 'I think you can call that sex.'

'God,' I say, my face heating.

She laughs. 'I'm really happy for you, you know.' She reaches a hand out and it lands on my thigh, next to my phone. 'I mean, it would be better if I could see you. But I'm happy for you that it's going well with Alex. And that you are getting, you know, off.'

I snort. 'Thank you. What about you? How's Liam?'

'Oh!' she says, pulling her legs up and crossing them. 'I didn't tell you! He's into edging.'

I shake my head. 'I don't know what that is.'

'Getting almost there and then… not.'

'That's a thing?'

'Yeah. And he's good at it.' Her eyes are shining and her cheeks are flushed.

'Is that for him or for you?'

'Well, it was for him at first. But then it went so well that we tried it with me as well and… oh my god.'

'Yeah?'

She shakes her head, her eyes closing. 'Possibly the best orgasm of my life.'

'God,' I say. 'It's a whole new world.'

'It really is,' she says.

'So how's it going out of bed?' I ask her.

She frowns. 'Do you know what? I like him.'

'That's not so weird,' I say. 'He sounds nice.'

She nods. 'But you know nice doesn't usually do it for me.'

That's true. As long as I've known her she's been drawn to the boys I was totally intimidated by. The boys she never knew where she was with. Bad boys, I guess.

'So what's changed?' I ask her.

'I think, maybe...' She holds her hands up in front of her. 'Don't start.'

'Ha!'

'It could be because of what happened with Rob. I think maybe I would like to try being with someone who really likes me, you know. I mean, all the time. As a person. Not just for sex.'

'That sounds like a radical idea.'

'Shut up,' she says. 'But yeah.'

'So are you still seeing other people or—'

'Maybe not. Right now. I mean, I'm not ruling it out. And if I met someone else tomorrow, I don't know. But right now... no. I'm okay just seeing him.'

'Wow,' I say.

'I know.' She smiles and then rubs her hands over her face. 'God.'

'I think this is the first time I've ever heard you say something like that.'

She shakes her head. 'Nope. Marc.'

'Oh god.'

When we first moved to London, Tash worked with this guy who was, I thought, a total dickhead. He couldn't seem to make up his mind whether he liked her or not. Or, at least, that's how he acted. He'd stand her up and then turn up in the middle of the night at the flat we were sharing. I hated him. Tash was utterly smitten. He was all she could talk about. The sex was amazing, but he treated her like crap and she fell desperately in love with him.

'He tried to add me on Facebook,' she says now. 'Did I tell you?'

'Fuck! No!'

'I didn't accept. Had a quick look at his photos. He's married. Poor cow. And he doesn't look that great.'

'He never did,' I say.

That was another weird thing about Marc – physically he wasn't Tash's type at all, she'd always gone out with the best-looking boy in any group. It was guaranteed that if I saw a boy and thought, *Hello!*, he'd be on his way to talk to Tash. But Marc was only okay-looking. Not bad-looking, but nothing special. And he had really stupid hair.

'So you and Liam?'

'We're going out tomorrow night, actually.'

'That's great,' I say. 'I'm really happy for you.'

'I wanted to ask you a favour,' Tash says. 'Will you come? I want you to meet him.'

'I… how?'

'If you just come too – we're going to a bar. And you can see him, watch him a bit… It's not going to be just the two of us, there's a couple of his friends coming too. Just… I don't want to make the same mistake again, you know? I want to be sure this time.'

'You want me to spy on him?'

'No! But yeah, maybe. A bit.'

'Okay,' I say. 'But I'm not getting dressed up.'

CHAPTER NINETEEN

The following night, we're waiting at the bus stop on Ranelagh Road. Tash looks gorgeous in a short black dress, ankle boots and a bright pink leather jacket. I'm wearing leggings, Uggs and a hoodie.

We've only been there a couple of minutes – Tash is leaning against the shelf thing and I'm standing in front of her so we can talk quietly to each other – when I see the men from the pub walking towards us. The men from the pub the night before all this happened: White Shirt, Dirty Jeans and Hipster Beard.

White Shirt isn't wearing a white shirt tonight – he's wearing a salmon pink polo shirt, but he still has sunglasses pushed up on his head. Dirty Jeans is still in dirty jeans. And dirty boots. And a dirty long-sleeved t-shirt. And Hipster Beard has added hipster ironic spectacles and a – for fuck's sake – fedora.

I stand very still, hoping they won't see me. And then I realise that of course they can't see me. But they can see Tash. And they do.

'Alright, gorgeous?!' Salmon Pink Polo Shirt shouts.

Tash ignores him, raising one eyebrow at me.

'Oy!' SPPS shouts. 'I've seen you before, haven't I?'

'I don't think so,' Tash says, without turning to look at them.

The three of them have stopped just to the side of the bus stop. They're standing in a row, blocking the pavement.

'I think so,' Dirty Jeans says. 'In the pub. Yeah?'

'No,' Tash says. Her face is completely blank. She looks bored.

Hipster Beard takes a packet of cigarettes out of his pocket and holds one out to Tash. 'Smoke?'

'I don't,' she says.

'Shame,' SPPS says. 'I bet you look good sucking on something.'

Tash rolls her eyes dramatically.

'Down on your knees,' SPPS says.

'Seriously?' Tash says. 'You need better lines.'

'We could go and do some lines, if you want,' Hipster Beard says.

Dirty Jeans says something I don't catch, but from the way the three of them laugh, it was something gross.

'Come on,' SPPS says to Tash. 'Come and have a drink with us. Don't be a bitch.'

'I'm not being a bitch,' Tash says, finally turning to look at them. 'And I don't want to have a drink with you. I'm waiting for a bus. Kindly fuck off and let me do it in peace.'

Dirty Jeans snorts, but I don't like the look on SPPS's face. For a second, I feel fear clench in my stomach. Tash is alone at the bus stop. Alone with three men. Even though it's a busy road, I'm not convinced anyone would stop if something happened.

'What did you say?' SPPS says.

I look around and think about going for help. Could I use Tash's phone? If I go and hide behind a wall—

'Just leave it, eh?' Tash says. 'You know I'm not interested.'

And then I realise. And I feel like a complete idiot. I don't need to go for help. I can totally deal with this myself.

'I think you are,' SPPS says. 'I think you'd like to come to the pub with us. I think you look like a right dirty bitch.'

The other two laugh. Dirty Jeans actually grabs his crotch. Who are these dickheads?

I perch on the shelf next to Tash and lean against her so she knows I'm there.

'It's okay,' she says, under her breath.

But it's not. Of course it's not. Usually, if something like this happened, I know I'd be scared and Tash would probably give them a load of shit and then they'd eventually fuck off and we'd be shaken and wouldn't feel better until we were in the pub with a drink.

'What?' SPPS says to Tash. 'Did you say something?'

But today it doesn't need to be like that. Today, I can actually give them a taste of their own medicine.

'No,' Tash says. 'I'm just waiting for the bus.'

I squeeze Tash's arm and walk around the outside of the bus shelter, being careful of the traffic. I walk up behind the three men and reach up to knock Hipster Beard's stupid fedora off his stupid head. It flies forward and he turns around and looks directly at me, a confused expression on his face. I suck in my breath – this would be a really bad time to become visible – but he's just looking to see what knocked his hat off, he clearly can't see me. He bends down to pick it up and I swing my leg back and kick him up the arse.

He stumbles forward, arms flailing, clearly trying to regain his balance, but he doesn't manage it and he falls heavily to his knees.

'What the fuck?' SPPS says.

'Was that you?' Hipster Beard says, on his hands and knees, turning round to look at the other two men over his shoulder. I think about kicking him again, but instead I nip through the gap between the other two and stand in front of SPPS.

'Get up, you prick,' SPPS says.

Hipster Beard picks his hat up and puts it back on his head while he's still on the ground and it falls off again as he clambers back up to standing.

'What the fuck are you laughing at?' SPPS says.

I look at Dirty Jeans, but he's not laughing, so I turn to look at Tash. She's not laughing, but she is smiling, her hand up and her fingers in front of her mouth.

'Stupid bitch,' Hipster Beard says as he finally gets himself upright again.

'You can suck my dick,' SPPS says.

'I don't think so,' Tash says. She's not smiling any more. She looks back down the street, past me, and I turn and see that the bus is coming.

Tash stands up, ready to signal the bus, and Dirty Jeans grabs her arm.

'Get your hands off me,' Tash says. Snarls, in fact.

'What did you fucking say?' SPPS says. Also snarls, actually.

I glance back at the bus and then I kick SPPS hard in the balls. Actually I don't. I don't quite manage it, I hit him mid-thigh, but as he yells, 'What the fuck?!' I kick him again and this time I hit the bullseye. He drops to his knees, both hands cradling his crotch. Dirty Jeans lets go of Tash to see what's happened to SPPS and Tash says, 'Izzy!' and steps to the edge of the kerb to signal the bus.

The bus stops and I grab Tash's hand and she pulls me on behind her. She heads straight up the stairs and I follow. I can see her shoulders shaking and I'm scared that she's traumatised. I can't wait to get upstairs so we can sit down and I can tell her everything's okay. But as soon as she sits down – in the seat directly opposite the top of the stairs – she turns to me and I see that she's crying with laughter.

'Oh my god,' she says, scooting along the seat and pressing her head against the window to look down at the bus stop. 'I can't believe—'

I slide into the seat behind hers so that I too can look out of the window. The three men are still there, of course. SPPS is standing again, but bent over, as if he's winded. The other two are looking around with completely baffled expressions, as if it's suddenly about to become clear who exactly hit them.

My hands are shaking and I curl them into fists. I've never hit anyone before, I don't think. It felt good. That's probably bad.

'You were so fucking amazing,' Tash says. 'Where are you?'

There are other people on the bus, but they're all studiously ignoring Tash. Either that or they just assume she's on the phone.

'Here,' I say quietly.

'Come here,' Tash says. 'You mad cow.'

I move round and sit next to her and she hooks her arm through mine, squeezing me against her. I rest my head on her shoulder. I think the adrenaline's wearing off and I feel like I might cry.

'You were so great,' Tash says. I can feel her breath on my face. 'You were like a superhero.'

I snort. 'Yeah, right.'

'You were. You made them look like the total arseholes they are. I hope that polo shirt dickhead's balls don't come down for a week.'

I laugh. But I'm still shaking.

'How did it feel?' Tash asks quietly.

'It felt really good,' I tell her. 'I was almost disappointed when the bus came. I wanted to grab two of them by the ears and bang their heads together.'

Tash barks out a loud laugh. 'That would have been excellent. Maybe next time, eh?'

She squeezes my arm again and I rub my head against her shoulder.

'Were you scared?' I ask her.

'Yeah,' she says. 'A bit. I mean, I don't think they'd do anything, but it's still... Even being spoken to like that is scary.'

'Yeah,' I say. I picture their faces, the way they were looking at Tash, as if they knew they could say or do anything. That kind of arrogance is terrifying.

'Were you?' Tash asks me.

'I was at first.' I look past her, out of the window, at the shop signs blurred through the smudged glass. 'But once I realised I could do something... no. I was thinking about going for help. And scared I wouldn't find anyone. When I realised I could help us myself, it felt—'

'Powerful?' Tash suggests.

'Not really, no,' I say. And then, 'A bit.'

'I would think,' Tash says. 'You know what it reminded me of?'

'What?'

'That scene in *Thelma & Louise* when they shoot that guy's truck.'

I laugh. 'Oh shit. Yeah.'

'Who knew you were picking up tips?' Tash says. 'I thought you were just thinking about Alex.'

I elbow her in the side and she squeezes me again.

CHAPTER TWENTY

'Where's the bar?' I ask Tash when we get off the bus at the bottom of Tottenham Court Road.

'Not sure,' she says. 'Somewhere round here.' She's got her phone in her hand and she's turning in a circle, trying to work out where she is on the map. 'Let's try over there.' She hooks her other arm through mine again and I let her tug me along.

'How's this going to work?' I ask her. 'How are you going to talk to me?'

'I'll just talk to you,' she says, shrugging. 'Or I'll use my phone. It's probably going to be loud in there anyway. Don't worry about it.'

'Isn't he going to think it's weird? Liam?'

'He probably won't notice,' she says. 'I think some of his friends are going to be there too, he'll be talking to them. It'll be fine.'

'Here we go,' she says. The bar has seating outside, a few people sitting, smoking, but I follow Tash to the door and inside.

'You okay?' she says into her phone.

'I'll feel better when I've had a drink,' I tell her.

'Tell me if you want to leave, yeah? Hang on a sec…'

We step to the side while she texts Liam to tell him we've arrived – I mean, *she's* arrived. The bar is huge, with high ceilings dotted with chandeliers, a large glass bar running all the way down one side.

'He's on his way,' Tash tells me. 'Let's go and find a seat.'

Tash tugs me into a booth, behind a kidney-shaped glass-topped table and under yet another chandelier – this time a 'modern' one made of wine glasses.

'What does he look like?' I ask her as she pulls her coat off and drapes it over my lap. 'Liam?'

'Hang on,' she says. 'Just checking if that looks weird.'

She stands up and takes a couple of steps before coming back and perching on the edge of the seat next to me.

'Nope, just looks like a coat on a seat. Excellent. What do you want to drink?'

'Anything I can drink with a straw,' I say. 'And Liam?'

'He's gorgeous,' she says, shrugging. 'I'll whistle if he comes in while I'm at the bar, don't worry.'

'Gorgeous,' I mutter to myself. 'Helpful.'

I suddenly feel self-conscious and tug at my top until I realise I'm actually making it visible and I have to sit on my hands instead. Oh yeah. The invisible thing. I don't need to feel self-conscious in front of Liam and his presumably equally gorgeous mates. It's odd how long it's taking me to realise that. Or maybe it's not.

I suppose I've felt self-conscious like this since I was about ten, so I shouldn't be surprised that it's taking more than a couple of weeks for it to wear off. I wonder if when I become visible again – assuming I do – I'll go back to feeling exactly the same as before. Or if it'll have some sort of long-lasting effect.

I hear Tash whistle and it makes me laugh – she used to do that when we were teens. I look up and she gestures at the door. When I look over I see three people walking through the bar towards Tash. There's a white guy with cropped hair and nice eyes. He's wearing a black polo neck and black trousers and I don't think he can be Liam. Behind him is an Asian guy with huge eyes, long eyelashes, a pouty mouth and incredible cheekbones. I murmur 'Holy shit' under my breath. That's definitely Liam. God.

Although I'm not sure it can be because he's holding hands with a white girl with ombre hair, a pierced nose and a bored expression. I watch as Tash hugs and air-kisses them all, then she comes and sits down next to me, putting two drinks on the table. They're both tall with mint sprigs sticking out of the glass, lime wedges curled over the side and straws.

'Mojitos,' she murmurs. 'It's Happy Hour. Perfect.'

Still looking over at the three people at the bar – the girl is standing in front of the hot boy now, his hands on her waist – I reach out and pick my drink up.

'Iz!' Tash hisses, grabbing the glass out of my hand and putting it back on the table.

'Shit,' I say. 'Sorry, I forgot. I'm just… Which one's Liam?'

'The one all in black,' Tash says out of the corner of her mouth.

I frown. He's definitely good-looking, but nowhere near as hot as Tash usually goes for. And frankly, next to the Asian guy he looks fairly ordinary.

I lean forward and suck my drink through the straw.

'What?' Tash says.

'I didn't say anything.'

'That's my point.'

I sit back up again and lean against her so she knows where I am.

'He's just… he's not quite what I was expecting.'

'How?'

'I don't know,' I say. 'Tell me who the other two are. Quick, before they get back.'

'Ravi,' she says, her mouth barely moving. She's getting good at this. 'And Gemma. They're a couple. Ravi's Liam's best mate.'

I don't get a chance to say anything back because the three of them come and join us, carrying two drinks each.

'This was a good shout,' Liam says to Tash, dropping onto the seat next to her, and holding up his two cocktails before putting them down on the table.

'Hey,' he says then, smiling at her. He leans forward and kisses her gently, before leaning back, still staring at her. He looks completely smitten. He's not at all what I was expecting.

Ravi and Liam start talking about work and Gemma leans past them to ask Tash about her work. Gemma's a freelance beauty writer and apparently she and Tash have already talked about some opportunities with a company Tash is doing PR for. I watch them and occasionally lean down and take another slurp of my drink when no one's looking.

By the time I've finished my drink, the bar is significantly more crowded, the music is louder, and Gemma's pulled a stool around so she can sit on the opposite side of the table, making it easier to talk to Tash.

Obviously no one's talking to me and I can't talk to anyone either, but I'm not at all bored. I can watch people without them knowing I'm watching and I like it. It's nice to just hang out and relax without worrying that people are looking at me or what people are thinking of me. Liam goes to the bar for more drinks, bringing two for everyone again, and then Gemma stands up.

'I'm just going to the loo,' she says, leaning down and picking her bag up from under the table. 'You coming, Tash?'

'Yeah, actually,' Tash says. She bumps me with her hip and I slide to the end of the seat and stand up. As she passes me, she squeezes my arm.

'I really don't get the whole going to the loo together thing,' Ravi says.

Gemma rolls her eyes. 'Even though I've told you more than once?'

Ravi grins up at her. He really is staggeringly handsome. 'Tell me again?' he says.

'Nope,' Gemma says. 'Use your imagination.'

'Oh fuck, don't say that,' Tash says. 'He'll think we're going to hook up.'

'Oh for fuck's sake,' Gemma says.

'No,' Ravi says. 'Don't say anything else. Just go. Go and let me be happy with that mental image.'

'Perv,' Gemma says, but she's looking at him fondly.

The two of them leave and I wonder if I should go with them – if that would be easier or if it would be easier for me to go on my own.

'Why do they go together?' Liam asks Ravi.

'Safer, innit?' Ravi says.

'God,' Liam says. 'That's fucked up.'

'Not just that,' Ravi says. 'Also for, like, sharing tampons and shit.'

Liam drinks some of his lager then says, 'I really like her.'

'I know, man,' Ravi says. 'And Gems likes her. And you know what Gems is like. She fucking hates everyone.'

Liam laughs. 'She doesn't. She's great.'

'Tash seems great,' Ravi says.

'She is,' Liam says, leaning forward and picking up his drink again. 'She's amazing. And fucking hell, she's unbelievable in bed.'

Ravi laughs. 'Don't. I'm struggling not to think about them hooking up in the loos right now.'

'Fuck,' Liam says, his mouth dropping open. 'Yeah.'

Ravi punches him in the arm. 'That's my girlfriend, man.'

He reaches into his pocket and pulls out his phone – the screen lit up with a message. He apologises to Liam and starts texting. Liam turns to face me and I hold my breath. He's looking straight at me, a tiny line between his eyebrows, and then he reaches over and grabs Tash's jacket. His fingers brush my thigh and I shuffle away, involuntarily, but he doesn't seem to notice. He smooths Tash's jacket with his hand and then puts it down on the seat next to him.

All sorts of things are going through my head – was he checking for her phone or her purse? But he's kind of brushing the jacket with his thumb and I decide he just actually wanted to touch something of hers. I can't decide if that's sweet or creepy. But he likes her. And he said nice things about her when she wasn't there. That's good.

Tash and Gemma come back and Tash picks her jacket up and drops it over my lap again. Liam kisses her on the neck as she sits down and she sort of curls into it, which surprises me – Tash has never really been into PDA. I remember when we were teenagers, the two of us went out with these two boys. Her boy put his arm round her almost as soon as we set off and she hit the roof, calling him disrespectful and shoving him away. I thought she was such a badass.

I was always embarrassed to tell boys not to touch me if I didn't want to be touched. I think back to kissing Marco when I bought that muffin. Have I not actually changed at all? I'd like to think I wouldn't let someone touch me if I didn't want to be touched, but I'm not sure I would. I'm such a wuss, it's ridiculous.

I feel Tash bump me again and I realise she's getting up again.

'We're going to dance,' she murmurs.

I sit back down and then I realise I want to go and dance too. The bar is crowded enough that even if I bump into people they're not going to notice. And, again, they're much more likely to think it's down to the crowd, not that an invisible person is dancing nearby. I follow Tash and Gemma to the back of the bar where the dance floor is. It's already packed. Nineties R&B has been playing since we arrived and Tash and Gemma immediately start doing the bent knee, head back, arms swinging thing, right next to each other.

I stand nearby for a second, feeling self-conscious even though no one can see me, but then I think *fuck it* and I start to dance. And it feels amazing. I'm not looking around to see if anyone's judging me or thinking about coming to dance with me or looking like they might want to make a move, I can just dance and not give a shit.

I can't remember the last time I danced just for the joy of it and that briefly makes me feel sad, but I decide I can think about that tomorrow. I really want to enjoy what is happening right now.

I twirl round, I hold my hands over my head, I throw my head back. I start to sing along and then stop, panicking that someone will hear me, but when I look around, everyone else is focused on their own dancing, their own dance partner. No one's taking any notice of me. So I carry on singing.

'Jumpin', Jumpin'' by Destiny's Child is playing and for a second I feel a pang of disappointment because Tash and I have a kind of routine to this song. It only really involves jumping during the chorus, but we always end up in fits of laughter. I swing around, smiling at the thought of it and see her teaching it to Gemma, who is already doubled over laughing. I want to grab Tash and tell her I'm here, that she can do it with me even though she can't see me, but that would be mad so I don't. By the time the next chorus comes round, Tash and Gemma are both Jumpin', Jumpin' and by the end of the song, Liam and Ravi have joined us.

I don't know the next song, but it's slightly slower. Ravi grabs Gemma's hips and they spend the entire track grinding against each other. They look really good together and so sexy I can hardly stand to look at them. Liam is dancing closer to Tash, but not actually against her. I see him slide his hand down her arm and twist his fingers with hers and she slides her hand round his back, pulling him closer. He's smiling at her and singing along with the music and even though he's not the best dancer – he seems a little stiff and self-conscious – he looks good because he looks so besotted with Tash.

It makes me miss Alex. I wish he was here. I wonder if he can dance. To real music, not just a Super Mario theme he's singing himself. I smile at the memory. But then picture him here, looking like he's dancing with nothing. That really wouldn't work. But still. I wish he could be. I step off the dance floor and move around the edge, towards the loos, pulling the door open the smallest amount I can fit through and then dodging into the first available cubicle. I pull my phone out of my vest and tap on Alex's name. I realise that I can talk out loud here. If no one can see me, no one can tell I'm invisible. Ironic. It feels oddly freeing.

'Hey, hi,' Alex says in my ear.

'Hi,' I say back. 'I'm at a bar. With Tash. And this guy she's seeing. And their friends.'

'Oh wow,' Alex says. 'How is it?'

'It's good, actually. Weird. For obvious reasons. But good. What are you doing?'

'Just watching a movie on my laptop.'

'Nice,' I say. I take a deep breath. 'I miss you.'

'I miss you too,' he says. 'I'll see you tomorrow?'

'Hope so, yeah. I'll let you get back to your film.'

He laughs. 'It's not that good. But thanks.'

I flush the loo and then open the door carefully. There's a group of women in front of the mirror, talking and laughing and reapplying their make-up. One of the taps is running, so I hold my hands under it quickly and then turn to the dryer before anyone has a chance to see anything.

As I open the door to the bar, the door to the men's opens and a bloke walks out, wiping his wet hands on the back of his jeans. Funny how the ladies' is always full of women reapplying make-up, doing their hair, fixing their clothes, whereas the men just pee and go.

I can't see Tash or the others on the dance floor. I make my way over to our seats, dodging out of people's paths. I bump into one guy, jogging his arm and the two drinks he's holding. He says, 'What the fuck?' but doesn't even turn to look. When I get back to where we were sitting, the table's surrounded by people laughing and doing shots. I manage to manoeuvre myself next to Tash and curl my fingers around her wrist.

'Fuck!' she says, glancing down. 'Izzy!'

'Who's Izzy?' Liam says, looking past Tash and right at me.

'My friend,' Tash says. 'I thought I saw her. But it wasn't her.' She sort of staggers forward and plants her mouth right on his. I see his eyes widen, but then he sits down, pulling her down onto his lap. I let go of her wrist.

There are more cocktails on the table, so I drink most of another one and then, when Tash and Liam still haven't come up for air, another. I take out my phone and put it on the seat next to me, glancing around to make sure no one's watching. I text Alex *If the film's not that good, you could come and find me?* along with the address of the bar.

I see Alex as soon as he walks in. He's wearing black jeans and a white shirt and I want to unbutton it and slide my hands inside.

'Hey!' Tash says, looking happy and blurry. 'Alex is here!'

Smiling back at Tash, Alex sits down next to me and I tangle my fingers with his, resting my forehead on his shoulder.

'You came,' I say against his neck.

'How could I resist?' he says, his voice low.

'We should go and dance!' Tash says, pulling Liam to his feet again. He looks shell-shocked, but he goes willingly.

'You okay?' Alex asks, his mouth close to my ear.

I wonder about dragging him off to the loos with me, but instead I say, 'Do you want to dance?'

The rest of the night is music and lights and drinks full of ice and leaves. I drink and dance and drink and dance until I'm dizzy and I feel like I'm dreaming. Alex holds my hand and I press up against him and I wish I wasn't invisible because I want him to be able to touch me and kiss me and he can't.

I'm at the edge of the dance floor, swaying to a slow song, watching Gemma and Ravi holding each other, his mouth on her neck, her hand in his hair, when I hear Tash say, 'Izzy?'

I turn round. She's right next to me. She's got her phone in her hand.

'I'm here,' I say, touching her arm.

'We're leaving,' she says. 'Me and Liam. Can Liam come back to ours? Otherwise I don't know how—'

'S'fine,' I say. 'I just need to pee again. I can sleep on the sofa. You can fuck him in my bed.'

Tash laughs and holds a finger up towards my lips, actually poking me on the chin. 'Shhh!'

'I'll go back to Alex's,' I say.

'Is that okay?' Tash asks Alex. 'Can Iz go home with you?'

He frowns for a second, then says, 'Yeah. That's fine. Have a good night.'

CHAPTER TWENTY-ONE

'I don't think we can go to my place,' Alex says, once we're outside. There's no one around – the shops and cafes are closed. The road is still busy, but the cars, buses and taxis aren't going to notice Alex talking to himself.

'Why not?' I ask, pressing up against him, dipping my lips to the soft spot where his neck meets his shoulder. 'Not allowed to bring girls back? That's the beauty of me being invisible…'

He laughs and kisses my temple. 'No. That's not it.'

He lights a cigarette, turning to blow the smoke away from me.

'Then what? You've been to my place a bunch of times. I want to see where you live. Is it a creepy serial killer type place? Or have you got My Little Pony wallpaper? Oh wait, are you married?'

I say it as a joke, but as soon as the words are out of my mouth, my stomach plummets.

'Oh my god, you're not, are you?'

'No!' Alex says, one hand tangling in the back of my hair as he tips my face up. 'God, no, of course I'm not married.' He kisses me quickly and I feel some of the tension leach out of my shoulders.

'I…' he says and then stops. And I feel his lips on the top of my head, his fingers pressing between the bones on the back of my neck. 'It's…' he says.

'What?' I say. 'It can't be that bad. Just tell me.'

'I think,' he says, his voice is wobbling as if he's nervous and it makes me nervous too. But it also makes me want to tell him it's okay. 'I think it'd be better if I showed you.'

'Okay,' I say, moving my hand down to tangle with his. 'And, honestly, I don't even mind if it is the My Little Pony wallpaper. We've all been there.'

He grins. 'No My Little Pony wallpaper, I promise.'

'Is it far?'

He shakes his head. 'Nope. It's actually really near.'

'That's good,' I say. 'Short commute.'

He huffs out a laugh. 'Yeah.'

We walk up Charing Cross Road and turn down Manette Street and then right on Greek Street.

'Wow,' I say, swinging our arms a bit. 'You live really close to work.'

And then we walk into Soho Square and right up to the office.

'We're going to the office,' I say. I'm really confused.

Alex looks nervous. He's biting his lip and squeezing my hand and when he slides the key card into the door his fingers are shaking.

He doesn't speak as we walk up to the office.

'Is this 'cos you want to do it on Mel's desk?' I ask eventually, because I can't stand the tension. 'You could've just asked.'

He laughs, but doesn't say anything, just leads me through the office – which is almost entirely dark apart from the light from a few computers that haven't shut down properly – and to the archive room.

'Alex,' I say as he opens the door and gestures for me to go inside.

He turns the light on. 'Just let me show you, okay?'

His cheeks are pink and he lets go of my hand and then runs his hands back through his hair. He pulls the stepladder down from the hook at the end of the row of files and climbs up a couple of steps, taking a box down from the top right hand corner of the metal shelving. He steps back down, puts the box on the floor and takes off the lid.

I'm expecting to see the green hanging files that fill the rest of these boxes, but instead I see fabric. I can't tell what it is, but Alex leans over and lifts it out. It's navy and orange and shiny and unmistakably a sleeping bag.

'Alex,' I say, my voice barely more than a whisper.

He doesn't even look at me; he bends again and lifts out a pillow, a bed roll and a washbag.

'Alex,' I say again, louder this time.

He looks at me and his eyes are wide and almost scared. 'So,' he says. 'Now you know.'

I can't move. I can't think. I want to fling myself at him. I want to press myself against him. I want to kiss that expression off his face. I breathe in and out.

'Izzy?' he says, running his hand through his hair again. 'Say something. I can't—'

I don't. Instead I take two steps and press up against him. He's not expecting it, so he staggers back, bashing into the desk. I push my hands into his hair and pull him down to kiss me.

'I can't believe—' I say against his mouth. 'Why didn't you ever—'

He pulls me more firmly against him, settling back against the desk and moving his legs to make space for me between them.

'I thought...' he says as I drop my head back and he kisses down my throat. 'I was embarrassed. I thought you might not want to go out with me if you knew.'

I let out an involuntary honk of laughter and press my forehead against his shoulder. 'Alex. I'm fucking invisible. I'm in no position to judge.'

'Fair point,' he says, smiling and kisses me again.

I pull his shirt aside to kiss his collarbones – I love them – and then I pull back. 'Hey. Where are all your clothes?'

He smiles. 'Ah. Well for a start, I don't have many. I keep a jumper on the back of my chair in the office. I've got a couple of t-shirts in the drawers. And then there's some stuff in another box.' He points at the boxes above his head.

'Right,' I say and kiss him again, smoothing my hands down his back, his hands resting on my waist.

'That morning!' I say, pulling back again. 'When you were singing Super Mario!'

'Oh god,' he says. 'You heard that?'

'I did,' I say. 'I loved it.' I kiss him again.

'I mean,' he says, dipping his head to my neck. 'I probably would have told you sooner if I'd known archive rooms got you so hot.'

'So no one else knows?' I say.

'I think Mary suspects,' he says, talking about the cleaner. 'She's never said anything, but she gives me this look sometimes. But apart from her, no. Not as far as I know. I'm pretty careful.'

'So,' I say, resting the top of my head on his chest. 'Can I ask why?'

'Course. You can ask anything. I told you that I used to have a flat share? Well, that fell apart. Literally, the ceiling caved in. And the friends I was sharing with went travelling. And I didn't know anyone well enough to get a place together. And the rooms I looked at were stupidly expensive with huge deposits that I just didn't have. I don't get paid that much. I could never save anything. We didn't get all our deposit back from the first place 'cos we had this party and stuff got... broken.'

I squeeze him and his arms tighten around me.

'I kept looking further and further out from the office, but whatever I was saving on the room was costing me on the commute. I stayed in a hostel for a few nights, but then I thought about staying in the office until I could save up for a deposit and a couple of months' rent and... here we are.'

'I wish I'd known,' I say quietly.

'How would you have known?' he asks, smiling at me. 'And what would you have done?'

'I don't know. You could've come and slept on my sofa.'

'Max would've loved that.'

I roll my eyes. 'I just… Isn't it weird? Aren't you lonely?'

'Sometimes,' he says. 'I mean, I was. Before.'

'Before?'

'Before I found you,' he says.

My breath catches in my chest and I can't speak.

'Izzy?' he says, his voice wavering a little.

'That's… a lot,' I say.

'Is it?' He smiles and I want to jump up on him like a koala.

'Yes.'

'Oh,' he says, his mouth twisting in amusement. 'I didn't realise.'

I stare at him. I want to kiss him. But he sleeps here. He sleeps in the archive room. I can't believe it.

'Is there…' I drag my eyes away from his face and look around the room. 'Where do you sleep? Just right here?'

He shakes his head and I step back as he pushes away from the desk. I follow him to the 'L' part of the room and he slides the first filing cabinet out behind us.

'Privacy,' he says.

I shake my head. 'I still can't believe you've been sleeping here all this time. God, Alex.'

'It's fine, honest. But I'm seriously not expecting you to stay here.' He pulls his phone out of his pocket. 'There must be a hotel—'

'I want to,' I say, reaching for his phone. He laughs as I pull it out of his hand.

'You really don't,' he says.

'I do.'

'I've only got one sleeping bag,' he says.

I put my hands on his chest and kiss him gently. 'Not a problem.'

*

'Ow, sorry, that's my—'

'No, I'm sorry, I thought I—'

'It's okay. Just let me—'

'Yeah, that's better. I can feel where—'

'Just… if you put your hand here then—'

'Wait. Just let me—'

'Hang on. If you just sit, then I can—'

'Okay, yeah. Sorry. I just wanted to—'

It turns out that having sex on the floor in an archive room isn't all that easy or comfortable.

'That's good,' he says, smiling. 'I can feel you now.'

'Is it too much? Am I squashing you?'

'God, no. Don't worry so much.'

One hand slides up my back and the other into my hair and then we're kissing again and I'm pressing myself against him and I stop thinking. Or at least, I stop thinking about everything else. I think about Alex. About the way he smells and tastes and feels. About his hair in my hands, his skin under my fingers. I graze his earlobe with my teeth and rub my cheek along his jaw. His eyes are closed and his lashes are long and his lips are full and biteable. I bite them.

I move off him and lie back on the hard floor, guiding his hands back to my body. I pull his jumper over his head and run my fingers down his chest. He's more muscular than I expected – properly defined pecs and a hint of a six-pack. The line of hair running from his chest down behind the waistband of his jeans makes my breath catch.

His hands move up the front of my body, grazing my breasts and I arch my back.

'Let me take this off,' I mumble. 'Close your eyes though, 'cos it's going to look really weird. Like a magic trick.'

He grins. 'That sounds cool. Let me watch.'

'No. Shut your eyes.'

'What if I just shut one?'

I sit up and kiss him again. 'No. Shut them both.'

He does. He's kneeling up now, his eyes closed, smiling. I just want to look at him.

'Is it off?' he says, opening one eye.

'No!'

He closes his eyes again and I pull my t-shirt over my head and drop it on the floor next to the sofa and lie back down, pulling him on top of me.

We both groan as his chest touches mine and I hook one leg around his thigh.

'Oh god,' he says, against my neck. 'I wish I could see you.'

'I know. I'm sorry.'

'No, I'm sorry. I mean, pointless thing to say, I know. I just…' He kisses along my collarbone and traces his lips across my chest. 'You're just so beautiful.'

'Water!' I almost yelp. 'You could see me – a bit – with water.'

'Oh god, yeah,' he says. 'Let's do that.'

He stands up and bangs his head on one of the rails of files that must have slid out when he moved the cabinet.

'Shit,' he says. 'Hang on. I've got water in my bag.'

He slides the cabinet back and I hear him in the other part of the room, and then he's back. He puts his bag down in the corner and takes the top off a bottle of Evian.

'Will this work?' he asks, looking down at me.

'I think so,' I say. 'Are you going to… pour it on me?'

His eyebrows quirk up and my face gets hot.

He grins. 'Maybe not here – we've got to sleep on this floor – but definitely save that idea.'

'Shut up,' I say. 'So what are you going to do, then?'

His eyes go dark as he dips his fingers into the water and then reaches towards me. I guide his hand to my face and he runs his finger along my cheekbone. I see his eyes widen and he gasps.

'Did it work?' I say.

'A bit,' he says. He dips his fingers again, before tracing them across my forehead, down my nose, across my lips. And then over again. More. I watch his eyes as he looks at me. His pupils are wide. I can feel his breath on my face. It's the most erotic thing I've ever experienced.

CHAPTER TWENTY-TWO

I wake up suddenly and at first I don't know where I am. But the ache in my hips, the gentle snoring next to me and the buzz of a Hoover from somewhere nearby helps me orientate myself. The archive room. With Alex.

I blink my eyes open and push myself up on my elbows, stretching my legs and rolling my lower spine. There's no way to argue that the archive room floor on half a sleeping bag and under a fleece blanket was comfortable, but I actually don't feel too bad. Maybe the drinks helped me sleep. Or maybe it was the sex.

The sex. Alex is sleeping on his side with his back to me and the fleece blanket has fallen down to his waist. I run my finger from his shoulder down to his hip and he shivers, but doesn't stir. I shuffle forward and press my lips to the base of his neck and he makes a low sound.

'Hey,' I whisper.

He doesn't move.

I press myself up along his back, my arm around his waist, face against his neck. If the cleaner is here, it's probably only about six and we've got a bit of time before we have to get up.

Alex shuffles slightly and he tangles his fingers with mine.

'You awake?' I whisper.

Still nothing.

I think about waking up with Max. About how I had no urge to touch him, to kiss him, to hold him like this. I think about how different the sex was last night. How I had no idea it could even be like that. How ridiculous it is that I feel like Alex really sees me, even though I'm invisible.

My eyes fly open and I turn my head, twisting to make sure I am actually still invisible. I am. Relief floods over me. And then anxiety rushes after it.

When did I stop wanting to become visible again?

CHAPTER TWENTY-THREE

'Fuck!' Alex says, flipping onto his back and dislodging me from my position pressed up against him. 'What time is it?'

'I don't know. It must still be early.'

'Have you heard Mary?'

'Yeah, she was hoovering when I woke up.'

'Fuck,' he says again. 'I should've been up—'

He clambers to his knees and I reach out and run one hand down his thigh. 'Hey, wait.'

'I'm sorry,' he says. 'Shit, I won't be able to get a shower.'

He stands up and bangs his head on the file shelf again, before pulling his underpants and jeans on.

'Are you okay?' he asks me as he rummages in the pile of clothes we threw down last night. 'Iz? Are you okay?'

I'm sitting up now. 'Yeah. I'm good. I—'

'Fuck!' he says again. He's found his phone. 'It's eight o'clock.'

'Shit.' Even though our official start time isn't actually until ten, I know the office starts filling up from about eight.

'What can I do?' I ask. I grab my leggings – my knickers are still tucked inside – and pull them on, then stand up, managing to avoid the shelf.

'Just... help me tidy everything away,' Alex says. 'Shit, if anyone comes in...'

'Don't panic,' I say. 'People don't usually come in here, do they?'

'No,' he says, pulling his black jumper over his head. His hair flies up with static and I want to reach out and smooth it down, but instead I find my hoodie and pull it on. 'No, you're right. I just… I don't want anyone to…'

'I know,' I say. I reach out and wrap my fingers around his wrist and he turns and smiles at me, but it's slightly off. He's looking just past me. It makes something cold flutter in my stomach.

'Okay,' he says a couple of minutes later. All his stuff is back in the box. We've both got our clothes on. Last night's condom is disgustingly disposed of in the empty Evian bottle so that Alex can put it in his bag and not risk anyone finding it in here.

'I need to get to work,' he says. 'Are you okay to get home?'

'Yeah,' I say. 'I'm fine. Don't worry about—'

'Great,' he says. 'I'll call you later, okay?'

He slides the file cabinet back into position and heads for the door. He's almost there when he stops dead and turns back.

'Fucking hell, Iz,' he says as he crosses the room. He stops in front of me and this time he's looking directly at me. I relax for what feels like the first time since he woke up. 'I'm sorry. Are you okay?'

'I'm fine,' I say. 'Get to work.'

His arms wrap around me and his lips brush across my cheekbone.

'Last night,' he says.

'Was amazing,' I say.

'Yeah.'

I kiss his jaw.

'You'll be okay?'

'I'll be fine,' I say.

Once Alex has gone, I search around the archive room to make sure we haven't left anything behind. I find the vest top I've been wearing instead of a bra and roll it up and shove it inside the front pocket of my hoodie. Everything looks as it should, so I slowly and carefully open the door and step out into the office.

It's certainly not busy, but there are a few people around. Nichola – who, like me, started as an intern and worked her way up – walks almost right up to me, talking on her phone, not looking at me. I flinch and step back, banging into the door. She glances over, looking slightly surprised, but carries on to her desk.

I cross the office towards the bathroom and for the first time I actually miss being here. In the office. When I first started working here, I loved coming in and getting a coffee and checking my email. Everyone arriving, chatting, talking about what they'd got up to the night before, and then gradually we'd move on to whatever campaign we were currently working on. Insights frequently came out of those morning chats – as if the nugget of inspiration we'd been searching for was hiding and we couldn't find it until we stopped looking. It was exciting.

If I get back to normal and can come back to work in the office, I want to be more proactive. Mel once said that I just let the job happen to me – that I did what was expected of me, but nothing extra. If and when I get back, I want to make sure I do as much as I can. And I guess that starts with the pitch. I need to get home and work on it today. Time's running out.

I scroll through my phone as I sit on the loo.

There's a message from Tash from last night. It just says *Thk u* and then one that says *Lovy* which I think is meant to be 'love you'. I want to ring and tell her about last night. That Alex is homeless and lives in the office. That we had sex. But I can't do that from the office loo, so it'll have to wait. Instead I reply that I'm on my way home and hope that Liam will have left by the time I get there. That would be an awkward morning-after conversation.

I'm just about to open the door and head home when someone comes in and I have to wait them out. It's two people – I'm in the middle cubicle and they take one either side of me. There's unzipping and rustling sounds then one of them says, 'Have you heard anything from Izzy?'

Nichola.

'Nope,' someone replies. 'I know she took the Fancy Bantams files home – the old ones? 'Cos Mel was steaming.'

Debs. I don't know her very well. She only started here a few months ago but she and Nichola go to lunch together most days.

'I know,' Nichola says. 'She's trying to make out she's pissed off because she wanted the files, but you know it's actually 'cos they're in a mess.'

This is true. Mel definitely made some dodgy mistakes with the Fancy Bantams account, but everyone does, particularly when they're starting out. But I can imagine how stressed Mel's been about it when she knows the company could lose the account altogether.

'I don't know why she's worried, to be honest,' Debs says. 'It's not like Izzy's going to come up with anything.'

My head jerks up and for a second I worry that I've given myself away, before realising that's not possible.

'I know, right?' Nichola says. I hear loo roll scrolling and then she flushes and opens the cubicle door, her heels tapping on the tile floor.

I think the conversation's over, but no.

'Like, has she ever come up with anything good?' Debs says.

'Not really.' I hear the tap running. 'I mean, that's probably not fair. She's okay. She's come up with some solid stuff before, yeah. But that's not going to be good enough this time. We need something really brilliant. And she's just not up to that.'

I stare at the light under the cubicle door as Debs flushes and washes her hands. They both use the drier, still talking about the Fancy Bantams account, but not about me. And then they leave and it's quiet. And I'm left sitting on the loo, phone in my hand, thinking about how everything they've just said is right. But that it doesn't mean that I can't come up with something. Just because I haven't before. I already feel like there's something there I just can't get. Like it's on the tip of my tongue.

I jump as my phone buzzes in my hand. Mum. I decline the call, but it rings again immediately and then a text comes through: *THIS IS URGENT*

Shit. What if something's happened to Dad? Or to Mum and this is actually someone using her phone? (Although that text was definitely her style.) I answer, my voice echoing around the now empty bathroom.

'You haven't been paying the mortgage?!' she says. Or, rather, shrieks.

Oh god.

'It's complicated,' I say. 'And I'm sorry, but this really isn't a good time for me to talk.'

'I can't believe you would do this,' Mum says.

'I know,' I say. 'Mum, really, I can't talk now. And I'm sorry I didn't tell you. There's been a lot going on. With work. And Max moving out and—'

'We're going to come round. Tonight. Your father wants to look at your bank statements.'

That's not happening.

'No,' I say. 'I'm sorry, but I won't be there. And I need to go now. I'll call you later.'

'Where are you going? And you haven't forgotten about your father's party, have you?'

'Something for work. And no, of course I haven't. Don't come down, I won't be there. I'll call you, okay?'

'Fine,' she says. 'But I need to tell you that I'm—'

Someone comes into the bathroom, so I end the call. I've never done that before. It makes me feel slightly ill.

I bought the flat – on their advice – with money my gran, my dad's mum, left me when she died. The inheritance enabled me to put down quite a big deposit, but the mortgage is still more than I'd be able to afford, so I pay half and my parents pay half, the plan being that at some point I will sell at a profit and split the profits with them.

When Max first moved in, he was meant to pay the bills while I paid the mortgage, but he kept forgetting. Or cancelling the payments when he was skint with the intention of paying double the following month. But our cable kept getting cut off. So it seemed easier for him to be responsible for one payment – the mortgage – while I paid the rest of the bills. I don't know why I ever trusted him with it. I must've been a complete idiot.

As soon as I hear one of the other doors lock, I dart out of the cubicle and then back into the office. I'm halfway to my desk when I realise I've still got my phone in my hand. Thank god no one has noticed a phone travelling through the air on its own. I can't believe I'm actually fucking up being invisible. I push it inside my top, forgetting that I'm not wearing the stretchy vest, and it falls straight through and skitters across the floor towards Nichola's desk.

Shit.

'What the fuck?' she says, looking down at my phone.

She swings round in her chair and looks straight at me. I gasp and look down at myself to make sure I'm still invisible. And I am. She leans down and picks up my phone, pressing the Home button with her thumb. The lockscreen is a photo of me and Tash doing duck faces, so there's no way she's not going to know it's mine.

'Is Izzy here?' she calls to Debs, who sits a few desks away.

'I haven't seen her,' Debs says, shrugging.

Nichola gets up and crosses the office, still holding my phone. I follow her. I can't leave without my phone.

'Is Izzy here?' Nichola calls as she approaches Mel's office. Over her shoulder, I see Alex in the office with Mel.

'Is Izzy here?' Nichola says again, from the door.

Alex looks over at her. 'No?'

Nichola holds up my phone. 'Just found her phone. Someone dropped it. It was weird – there wasn't anyone there.'

'Maybe it fell out of a file or something?' Alex says, flushing pink.

'Yeah, maybe.' Nichola leans in the doorway, blocking my view of Alex. I take a couple of steps closer.

'It's funny 'cos I was just talking about her,' Nichola says. 'Me and Debs were wondering how she's been getting on with the pitch.'

'Alex and I were just talking about Fancy Bantams,' Mel says. 'He's got some good ideas.'

'Yeah?' Nichola says.

There's a short silence – I try to see Alex, but I can't without getting too close to Mel – and then I hear him say, 'You know the quote: "Why blend in when you were born to stand out?"'

My chest feels tight. I take another step. I'm too close to Nichola now, but I need to see Alex.

'People want to stand out,' he continues. 'They want to be seen – but not too much.'

I told him this. This is what I said I was working on. For the pitch.

'They want to feel like they're being seen,' Alex says. 'Without actually drawing too much attention to themselves. Does that make sense?'

I suddenly get an image of Alex and Nichola outside the office, smoking together. They were always smoking together.

'Absolutely,' Mel says.

I step backwards and bump into a chair. It knocks into the desk and some files fall over.

'What the fuck?' Nichola says again.

But I don't stop to look back. I head straight for the door.

CHAPTER TWENTY-FOUR

'Tash!' I shout as soon as I'm through the door.

The flat is bright with sunshine and I squint and then get myself a glass of water. I think I must be dehydrated. I can't think straight.

All the way home from the office, I went over and over what I heard Alex saying to Mel – interspersed with what Nichola and Debs said in the loo, and the worry that my parents will still come round – and there's no way I can make it mean anything other than he's trying to steal my idea.

'Tash!' I shout again, putting my glass in the sink and crossing the kitchen to push open my bedroom door.

'Oh fuck!' I say as soon as the door swings open.

Liam is lying on his back in the middle of the bed, arms up over his head. There's a Tash-shaped bump moving under the duvet.

'What the fuck?!' Liam says. He's looking at me, but he obviously doesn't know he's looking at me.

'Shit, I'm sorry,' I say, before I think better of it.

'What the fuck is happening?' Liam says, starting to scrabble up the bed.

The duvet flaps back and Tash sits up and looks over at me.

'Fucking hell, Izzy,' she says, pushing one hand back through her long hair that had been hanging almost entirely over her face. Her other hand is on Liam's chest and I can see it rising and falling with how quickly he's breathing.

'It's okay,' she tells him. 'I mean, you're not going to fucking believe it. But trust me, okay?'

He's staring at her, his eyes wide. He nods.

'Okay,' Tash says. 'Iz, go and make us some teas, yeah? I need to talk to Liam.'

'What the fuck?' I hear him say again as I leave the room and close the door behind me.

'You can touch me,' I say about ten minutes later when the three of us are sitting on the sofa – Liam at the far end and Tash in the middle. Three mugs of tea are steaming gently on the coffee table in front of us.

'Yeah,' Tash says. 'Hold your hand out.'

She's dressed now and she's tied her hair up in a messy bun on the top of her head. Liam's wearing the same clothes from last night and an utterly terrified expression.

Liam reaches his hand out in front of Tash and I touch her hand with mine. She picks my hand up and puts it on top of Liam's. He immediately yanks his hand back, then says, 'Shit. Sorry. Sorry.' He reaches out again.

'It's okay,' Tash reassures him. 'She won't hurt you.'

'Unless you hurt Tash,' I say. 'And then I might kill you.'

'Ignore her,' Tash tells him, rolling her eyes at me.

'I can't believe this,' Liam says. 'This is… did someone spike my drink?'

'That's what I thought when I woke up like this,' I say. 'But apparently not.'

'But this has got to be a prank, yeah?' he says. 'This can't happen.'

'I know,' I say. 'But it kind of has. Sorry.'

His hand feels soft in mine and I squeeze his fingers in what I hope is a reassuring, rather than terrifying manner.

'I think… I need to go,' Liam says, pulling his hand away again.

'Oh babe,' Tash says.

'Not because of… this,' he says. 'I mean, I need to go anyway.'

'Okay.'

Tash uncurls from the sofa and follows Liam to the door. They talk quietly for a bit and then Liam calls out, 'It was nice to meet you, Izzy. Sorry I didn't drink my tea.'

'What the actual fuck?' Tash says as soon as the door's closed behind him. 'Were you trying to give him a heart attack?!'

She flops back on the sofa next to me and picks up her tea.

'I'm sorry!' I say. 'I was freaking out. I forgot he was here.'

'Freaking out about what? Alex's place? Is it a sex dungeon? Has he got My Little Pony wallpaper?'

'Ha!' I say. 'That's what I said.' I reach for my own tea. 'No. I mean, he's homeless and living in the archive room at the office, but—'

'Oh shit,' Tash says.

'Yeah, that's not it.'

'Was the sex bad? Did you not have sex? Did he want to do weird stuff?'

'No, we did. And it was great. And I mean, I guess yeah to the weird stuff because I'm invisible and he had to put water on me to see me, but that's not it either.'

'Jesus Christ,' Tash says. 'Then tell me!'

'I've been *trying* to. Okay, so when I was leaving the office I overheard him talking to Mel and he was telling her stuff from my pitch. Like word for word. Stuff I told him. The only fucking thing I've managed to come up with. And he was telling her.'

'So?'

'So he wasn't saying "Oh, Izzy's come up with this, doesn't it sound great?" He was telling her as if it was his own idea. He was passing it off as his own.'

'You don't know that,' Tash says, frowning.

'Well it sure as shit sounded like it,' I say, my throat tightening. 'What if... what if that's been what he wanted all along? What if none of this has been real? What if he just wanted my job?'

Tash shakes her head. 'No. No way. I'm a better judge of character than that. I don't buy it. And I mean... surely there'd be an easier way. You're no picnic at the moment, you know. As much as I love you, there's no getting around the fact that you are fucking invisible.'

'I know,' I say. 'But... that makes it easier. For him. Because if this is permanent, then... I can't go back to work. He won't even need to take my job. It'll just be there, he can walk right into it.'

'You need to talk to him,' Tash says. 'Or Mel. You should talk to Mel. Give her everything you've got. Make sure there's no room for him to—'

'But it'll be his word against mine, won't it?' I say. 'And – and I know I'm repeating myself – but I'm fucking invisible!'

'Okay,' Tash says, leaning against me and rubbing her thumb over my elbow. 'Okay. We'll think of something. Just... drink your tea and calm down.'

'That's not even all of it.' I close my eyes and roll my head from side to side. 'My parents found out about the mortgage – that Max hasn't been paying it – and now they're freaking out. They were planning to come and see me tonight. I think I managed to convince them not to, but what if they'd just turned up? What the fuck would I have done?'

'You would have had to tell them what happened,' Tash says. 'What happened with Max?'

'Yes. But also what's happened with you.'

'That I'm invisible?!' I say, and I sound slightly hysterical even to myself.

'Yes.'

'As if.'

Tash laughs. 'But what else could you do? This isn't some West End farce. You couldn't, like, hide in your room and talk to them through the door, pretending you were contagious. You could just literally tell them.'

'It might kill them,' I say, biting on the edge of my thumbnail.

'We would cross that bridge if we came to it,' Tash says, and then grins at me. 'They're definitely not coming? 'Cos I'm thinking I'd quite like to see your mum's face…'

'She said they're not coming. But you never know with Mum. And I hung up on her, so—'

'Woah. You hung up on her?'

'Yeah. I mean the conversation was over and someone was coming into the loo, so I had to.'

'But still. Standing up to your mum. I'm all for it.'

I rub my face with both hands. 'It really sounded like Alex was stealing my idea.'

'I know it sounded like that to you,' Tash says. 'But I'm not sure you're the best judge. Have you called him?'

'That's another thing,' I say, flopping back against the cushions. 'Nichola's got my phone.'

'I think you got scared,' Tash says, once I've told her what happened with my phone.

I sigh.

'I know you, you know? Alex revealed this secret to you. And then you slept with him. And he told you that you're important to him. And god knows he's important to you.'

'What is this? "Previously on *Izzy's Ridiculous Life*"?'

'You got scared. And as soon as you saw an out, you took it.' Tash reaches over and pats at the air until I reluctantly take her hand. 'You didn't just take it. You grabbed it with both hands and legged it out of the office, shouting "A-ha!"'

'But why didn't he say it was my idea?' I say. 'He said "You know that expression?" He didn't say "Izzy told me about that expression".'

'Maybe Mel called him in there specifically to ask what you were up to? Maybe he'd already said that before you arrived? There are explanations, Iz. You don't need to jump to the worst conclusion.'

'But he shouldn't have been telling her my ideas, even if she asked.'

'Maybe not. But that's very different to "He stole my idea and that's the only reason he wanted to sleep with me in the first place", right?'

'Yeah,' I say. 'Fuck.'

I bang my head on the sofa cushion.

'You're falling for him,' Tash says. 'It makes sense that you're scared.'

'Are you scared? With Liam?'

'Fucking hell, are you joking? I'm terrified.'

'Really?'

Tash shakes her head, her hair swinging. 'He's just so... good. He's kind and hot and sweet and he's really into me. I keep wanting to tell him horrible things I've done. Or say, like, "You know I'm really fucked up, right?"'

'You're not fucked up.'

'I just... it feels too lucky. To have found him straight after everything that happened with Rob, you know?'

'You didn't find him after,' I say. 'You were already seeing him.'

She laughs. 'Yeah. But that was for sex. Not... feelings.'

I squeeze her hand. Fucking feelings.

'But you know what I mean?' she asks, squeezing back. 'Like this is what I said I wanted. And here it is. It feels like it's too soon. I'm just waiting for something to go wrong. I want to be all in. I think he's all in. But there's still this little bit of me thinking I'd better hold back in case I'm wrong.'

'Ugh,' I say.

'I know, right?'

I shuffle up the sofa so I'm sitting up straight. 'What were you doing? When I came in.'

Tash rolls her eyes. 'What do you think I was doing? Naked. In bed. With a man.'

'Yeah, I know. But I mean specifically. Were you doing something with your hair? It looked weird, when you sat up.'

She laughs. 'Oh yeah, he likes me to wrap my hair around his dick.'

'Of course he does,' I say. 'I can't believe I even asked.'

'Hey, listen, I think of the two of us, you're doing the kinkier shit at the moment.'

I huff out a breath. 'Yeah. I guess.'

'You just need to talk to him,' Tash says. 'Alex. I mean, I'm no expert, clearly, but I really think he's one of the good guys.'

Me too. At least, I hope he is.

CHAPTER TWENTY-FIVE

The next morning I open the door even though I know I shouldn't. Even though I am still invisible and it's going to scare the shit out of whoever's standing there. But it doesn't. Because it's Alex.

'Hey,' he says.

He looks tired; there are purple shadows under his eyes. He's wearing his black jumper and I want to fall against him, rub my face on his neck. But I can't.

'I've got your phone,' he says.

I don't say anything. We're still standing in the doorway.

'And I think I might've found a flat. It's only for three months, but it's something.'

'What?'

'I mean, it's a room. A bedsit. Not a flat. And I might have to sell a kidney at some point. But you can manage with one, right?'

'Why did you do that?' I ask.

He smiles from under his stupid floppy fringe. 'I mean, while the archive room floor sex was fantastic, I figured the novelty would soon wear off.'

'But... how did you pay for it?'

'I've been saving my wages all this time. But it turns out I don't earn enough to rent a cupboard. Literally. So I asked my dad to lend me some money. He's been offering, but I thought I was too proud. Turns out I'm not.'

'Okay,' I say. 'That's good.'

'Are you okay?' he says. 'Can I come in?'

I step out of the way to let him in and then remember he can't see that, so I say, 'Yeah. Sorry.'

I close the door behind him, but he doesn't come in any further.

'What's wrong?' he says. 'Has something happened?'

I take a breath. 'I heard you yesterday,' I say. 'I heard you talking to Mel.'

'Yeah?' he says.

And that's when I start to cry.

'Fuck,' he says. 'What?'

He reaches out and takes my face in his hands, his thumbs brushing over my tears, spreading them across my skin.

'I can't believe you would do that,' I say, my voice quiet.

'Do what?' he says. 'She asked me what you had. She was freaking out. You know what she's like. She said she'd tried to get hold of you. I wanted her to know you had it under control.'

I shake my head. 'You can't have my job.'

'Fuck,' he says. 'I don't want your job. Why would you think—?' He stares at me. 'You thought I'd stolen your idea? You thought I was trying to… you didn't think that I…'

He looks so shocked, so upset, that the tension I've been holding since I heard him talking to Mel just drains out of me.

'I really like you,' he says. 'I want to help you. At work. And anywhere else.'

'I'm sorry,' I say. 'I freaked out.'

'I'm not Max,' he says.

'I know,' I say. 'I just—'

'No,' Alex says, sliding his hands down my neck to my shoulders. 'I… I would never do something like that anyway. That's just not… that's not the kind of person I am. But I would never do anything like that to you. You're…' He shakes his head, frowning. 'In the archive room, when I said I was lonely before I met you... That's not... that really doesn't begin to explain how happy I am that I get to be with you.'

I want to say something. I want to tell him I feel the same way. But my throat's tight and I can't even speak.

'I think about you all the time. You're... I mean, you're invisible! It's ridiculous. But it doesn't matter. It hasn't mattered to me. Because everything I like about you, everything I know about you... I don't need to see you for any of that. You know?'

I shake my head. 'I'm sorry. I overreacted. I just... you're amazing. You're kind of too good to be true.'

Alex laughs. 'I get that a lot.'

I step forward and lean against him, the top of my head pressing against his chest. 'I freaked out.'

He strokes one hand back through my hair. 'That's okay.'

'I missed you,' I murmur against his jumper.

'I missed you too,' he says. He holds me for a second – I think I can feel his heartbeat, but it might be mine.

'Tash isn't here, right?' he says.

I laugh. 'No. She's at work.'

'Okay,' he says, smiling.

I tug him over to the sofa and push him down. He smiles up at me and I sit down, stretching my right leg over his left leg so I'm half in his lap. I brace my hands against his chest as I lean in to kiss him.

'Oh shit, yeah,' he murmurs against my mouth and moves his hands down to my lower back.

'I'm not giving you a lapdance,' I say, smiling.

He laughs, tipping his head back. 'You are in my head.'

I drag my left leg closer so that I am pretty much sitting in his lap. I can feel his erection pressing up against me and I curl my hips up slightly. He groans and moves one hand up into my hair, deepening the kiss. I let myself relax against him, my tongue sliding alongside his, and I finally close my eyes.

His hand is flat against my lower back, under my t-shirt, his skin warm against mine. His other hand runs through my hair as he breathes against my mouth.

'Shit,' I say, curving my hips up again.

'You feel…' he says.

I don't get to know how I feel because he's kissing me again and I keep my eyes open to watch him. His brow is furrowed and he looks like he's concentrating as he sucks gently on my bottom lip and I sigh into his mouth.

I lean back to look at him. His cheeks are flushed and his fringe is hanging down into his eyes. I want to push it off his forehead and maybe lick his eyebrows. Is that really a thing I just thought? Am I having some kind of breakdown?

'Shower,' I say, my voice cracking.

'What?'

'If we get in the shower—'

We can't get there quick enough. I strip off the rest of my clothes, leaving them on the floor behind me. Alex crashes into my bedroom door as he tries to take off his jeans before his shoes. I want to watch him, I want to look at him naked before we do this, but it doesn't seem fair. I want to look at him as he looks at me. I turn on the shower and climb in the bath, letting the hot water run over me. I feel it on every inch of my skin and I'm so turned on I can hardly stand it.

'Oh my god, Iz,' Alex says as he steps in after me.

I can't even speak. He looks perfect.

'Look at you.'

'You can see me?'

He smiles. 'You look like a goddess.'

'I know it's weird when the water runs off—'

He steps closer. 'It's not weird. Well, obviously it is a bit weird. But you're beautiful. It's so good to be able to look at you.'

I look down at myself. At the water running off my body. And I feel beautiful. I run my hands down my sides as Alex steps closer and I slide one hand round the back of his neck, pulling him into me, the water pouring over both of us until I don't know where he ends and I begin.

CHAPTER TWENTY-SIX

I can't stop thinking about 'Why blend in when you were born to stand out?' It goes round and round my head like an earworm.

People want to stand out. But not too much. Or they want to stand out, but only in ways they choose. I know there's something here. I just can't quite get at it. I Google. I read old customer interviews from the files Alex helped me bring home. I make a mind map. After waking up in the middle of the night and not being able to get back to sleep, I go for a walk. Alone.

It only takes me a couple of minutes to stop feeling nervous. No one can see me and so no one can threaten me. It's odd – my entire life I've just accepted that I can't go out after a certain time, that it wouldn't be safe for me to go out, alone, for a walk, at night. But why should that be the case? Why shouldn't I be able to do this? Why do we just accept that half the population basically has a curfew? That if I did this usually and something happened to me, people would say it was my fault for being out on my own at night? It's ridiculous.

I turn right onto Parkway and think about walking in the middle of the road, until I remember I'm invisible, not invincible. I keep walking, tipping my head back to look up at the dark sky, listening to the sound of traffic in the distance.

My shoulders prickle when I hear laughter and shouting and see a group of men and women coming round the corner. They're clearly drunk. The women are hobbling on their heels, hanging off the men's arms for support, the men are yelling to each other and one of them's singing something that sounds like 'Delilah', but it's so slurred and off-key I'm not really sure.

'Hey! Hey, love!' one of the men shouts and I freeze because he's looking directly at me.

'Hey!' he shouts again and I turn round and see a woman walking behind me. She's short and blonde and round and she's wearing wedge-heeled sandals and a nervous expression, her bag clutched under her arm.

I take a step back into the doorway of the Co-op and wait to see what he's going to do. I wish I could tell the woman that I'm here, that whatever he's planning isn't going to happen because I'm going to kick his arse, but I know she'd been even more scared of invisible me than she is of him.

The guy runs across the road towards us and I wonder at what point I intervene. The woman steps closer to me and I can smell her perfume, hear her breathing.

'You dropped—' the bloke says and he jogs a bit past us and then turns back, holding out a twenty-pound note.

'Oh!' the woman says. 'Oh my god! Thank you so much.'

'Alright, love?' the man says. He's got a Yorkshire accent. 'You don't want to lose a twenty, do you?'

The men on the other side of the road are jeering at him, the women laughing.

'Shut the fuck up, knobheads,' he calls back cheerfully. 'Are you alright?' he asks the woman. 'Do you know where you're going?'

'I'm just going to get a cab on the main road,' she says. She has an accent too, but I can't place it.

'Want me to walk you?' he asks, to more jeers from his mates.

'No,' she says. 'Thanks.'

He gives her a thumbs-up and jogs back across the road to cheers from the others. I walk behind the woman to the end of the road and wait until she's in a cab, watching it drive away until I can't see its lights any more.

I walk along Prince Albert Road, the direction her cab went, and wonder where she'd been and what she was doing out so late. I wonder what I would have done if the man had attacked her. I feel massive relief – and something close to joy – that he didn't. That he wanted to help. That she's going home feeling cheered by their interaction and not frightened or worse.

Hashtag not all men, as Tash would say. But enough men. That's the problem.

I look up at the huge, cream-painted houses that line the road and wonder about the people inside. Who they are, how long they've lived here, what professions allow you to own such beautiful houses in such an expensive part of London. There's a car parked outside one of them, half on the pavement, its boot wide open. I stop and look around, wondering if someone's emptying it and will be back out in a minute, but when no one comes, I reach up and try to slam it shut, but the catch is obviously broken and it springs open again.

There's not much in the boot – a child's scooter, a backpack, some loose books – but I want it to still be there in the morning, so I try to close the boot again, pressing on it instead of slamming it, but it springs open again. I think about going up to the house and ringing the buzzer, but I know some people have video entry phones now and I don't want to freak anyone out, so I carry on walking.

Will they come out in the morning and find the boot empty, their stuff stolen? Or will it all be as they left it and they'll feel like they had a lucky escape? I think about the blonde woman again – how it could have gone either way and there was just no way of knowing. That's the scariest thing.

I hesitate at the entrance to the canal – I can't walk along the canal at this time of night, surely. But then I realise that of course I can. I can go anywhere I want. It's even darker – there's no street lighting down here – but the full moon is surprisingly bright and

I turn on my phone torch, holding it close to my body. I doubt I'll bump into anyone down here at this time, but if I do, I can stick my phone back in my pocket before they realise what it is.

I've probably only been walking for about five minutes when I hear a sound that makes the hairs on the back of my neck stand up and my chest vibrate. A long, low, growl. A lion. Because somewhere in this park is the zoo. Once I realise, I can smell it: hay and manure and warm, ripe animal. It mingles with the scent of the canal, but then separates out and I can't believe I didn't notice it sooner.

I pass a geometric mesh aviary and hear chirping and tweeting. I look up and see a parrot hanging off the mesh. I can't see its colours in the darkness, but I can picture its bright blue and red and yellow feathers in my mind. I hear a sound from the other side of the canal, and I can see there's an animal enclosure there. I can't work out what it is at first, but I stare long enough that it gradually comes into focus. It's a giraffe and, once I see it, I can't believe I hadn't been able to see it sooner. It stares straight down the canal, its movements slow and languorous, long-lashed eyes blinking and enormous black tongue rolling out of its mouth to curl around a nearby branch, before scrolling back in again.

I don't know how long I watch it for, but by the time it turns and lopes back inside, I know exactly what I'm going to do for the presentation.

CHAPTER TWENTY-SEVEN

'How much coffee have you had?' Tash asks me. 'Did you even sleep?'

'Not much, to be honest.' I swirl the coffee in the bottom of my mug and finish it. 'I think I napped for a bit. But I was too excited.'

'I can't believe you went to the zoo in the middle of the night,' Tash says.

'Me neither. But it was amazing. Just being out there and not being scared was amazing.'

'I can imagine,' Tash says. 'I used to walk home on my own sometimes when I was at uni. There was this old guy who was always sitting on a fold-up chair in front of his house. I always looked out for him and we'd say hello. And then one night he said "I want to lick you all over" and I stopped walking after that.'

'Fuck's sake.' I stand up to make another coffee, then realise Tash is right and maybe I should have some water instead. 'That pisses me off. That's what I was thinking about last night.' I tell Tash about the guy with the twenty and how I was scared for the woman.

'The thing is,' Tash says, leaning back in her chair. 'Nine times out of ten... maybe more? Ninety-nine times out of a hundred? It's going to be fine. But you don't want to take that chance, do you? That's the problem. And all those times I walked home on my own and it was fine. But if anything had happened, people would have said it was my fault for being out on my own. It's fucked up.'

'I thought the same thing last night. And it just felt so good to be out there, you know? I'm so used to not being able to do it, I never even thought about it as a thing I should want.' I stretch my arms over my head and drink some water. 'Anyway. At least that's an upside to being invisible.'

Tash laughs. 'I think there are a few.'

I shake my head. 'I know. Is it awful that it doesn't even bother me any more? I mean, I'm worried about what's going to happen if I'm still like this by the time my dad's party comes round. But other than that…'

'There must be other things,' Tash says. 'Things you miss.'

'Well, work would be a problem, long-term, but I was mostly worried about the presentation and Alex is—'

'No, I don't mean that. I mean, like… I miss your face. Don't you miss your face? In the mirror? I think I'd miss mine.'

I frown. 'I don't think so? It feels like a relief not to worry about it, to be honest.'

'And clothes?'

'God, no. It's a massive relief not to worry about clothes. I can't believe I can just put any old shit on and no one knows or cares. I don't need to wear heels or Spanx or anything that doesn't feel good.'

'Forever, though? I can imagine that might be a relief for a bit – like if I'm ill and I stay in the same sad hoodie and leggings for days – but I'm always glad to get properly dressed and made-up again. Makes me feel more of a person.'

I shrug. 'I don't think so? Maybe it just hasn't been long enough yet.'

'Have you thought what you're going to wear for the presentation?'

I look down at myself and pull my t-shirt out so Tash can see it.

'No,' Tash says, pushing her chair back and standing up. 'What if you become visible again right before? You want to be in your scraggy clothes in front of everyone?'

I sigh. 'Probably not, no. Where are you going?'

'I'm going to see if you've got anything in your wardrobe.'

'I haven't,' I say, following her. 'There's nothing in there I want to wear.'

'Might give me something to work with,' she says, glancing at me over her shoulder as she yanks open my wardrobe doors.

'I forgot you were allergic to colour,' she says, flicking through my work clothes. 'Is this it? Really?' She closes the wardrobe doors.

'Pretty much,' I say.

'We need to go shopping.'

'But I won't be able to see how things look.'

'And that is why you'll have to trust me,' Tash says.

'God.'

'Come on. Get your coat.'

We've only been back at my flat for about twenty minutes when Alex comes round. I'd texted him when we were out, while I was bored out of my mind watching Tash choose clothes for me. 'What did you buy?' Alex says, pointing at the pile of bags on the sofa.

'I don't even know,' I tell him, wrapping my arms around his waist and letting him hold me.

'She lost interest,' Tash tells him. 'No stamina.'

'What's the point if no one can see her?' Alex says.

'Don't you start,' Tash tells him. 'Wine?' She holds a bottle up.

'Course,' Alex says.

Tash pours glasses for all of us and we take them over to the sofa.

'So what's the emergency?' Alex asks, after a few minutes.

'There's no emergency!' I say, rubbing my foot along the side of his leg.

He flinches at the touch of my foot and then grins at me.

'You sent me alarm emojis.'

I laugh. 'I told you what that was. I know what I'm going to do for the presentation. I wanted to send you a giraffe emoji, but there isn't one.'

'Right,' Alex says. 'Yeah, you're going to need to give me a bit more.'

'Not while I'm here, please,' Tash says, and then sips her wine.

I throw a cushion at her, but she knocks it to the floor before it gets close.

'What I was thinking,' I say. 'Was that I could do it for you – although obviously you're not going to be able to see it properly – just so you get an idea. And then maybe you could run through it, Alex?'

'No problem,' Alex says. 'Can I just have a cig first? Haven't had one all day. I ran out earlier and only just got a new pack over the road.'

I run my hand down his arm. 'Would you mind going outside? Instead of smoking out of the window, I mean? It's just… I could smell it last time and I don't—'

He bumps me with his shoulder. 'Course. You should've said.'

He leans down and kisses me on the top of my head before he lets himself out.

I look over at Tash, who's looking back at me with a very smug expression.

'What?'

'You've changed.'

'No shit. I'm invisible.' I drink some wine. 'I'm going to need your Photoshop skills.'

'Don't change the subject,' she says. 'You would never have asked Max to smoke outside.'

'Max didn't smoke.'

She rolls her eyes. 'If he had. You would've let him smoke out of the window even if it had made you sick. You would've put up with it. No matter what.'

'I let Alex smoke out of the window the first time he was here! But I could smell it on the cushions and stuff and if he's going to be here a lot, then I don't want—'

'I know,' Tash says. 'I get that. What I'm saying is that that is a new thing. For you. Saying "this doesn't work for me, can you do it another way" is a new thing. For you.'

I drink some of my wine. 'Maybe.'

'It is.'

'I think it's 'cos Alex is nicer than Max was and I knew he wouldn't mind.'

'Maybe,' Tash says, getting up to bring the wine over to the lounge. 'But mostly I think it's you.'

CHAPTER TWENTY-EIGHT

Alex is wearing a slim-cut navy suit with a white shirt open at the neck. He's clean-shaven and I keep wanting to kiss just under his ear where I know it drives him crazy. I have to resist. Today is too important.

From the side of the stage, we can see the podium in the centre, waiting for Alex to walk out and give the pitch. My pitch. We've rehearsed it over and over. Everything is ready, everything is perfect. Or it would be if I wasn't still invisible.

'I just wish I could do it,' I say. 'I know you've got it. I know you're going to be great, but—'

'I know,' he says. 'It's your baby. All your hard work. You should be the one to do it.'

'And I know you're going to be amazing.' I pick a bit of fluff off the arm of his jacket. 'But I just feel like I could really nail it, you know?'

'I know,' he says again.

And he is going to be brilliant. He's been brilliant every time we've run through it. But watching him say my words over and over just made me want to do it more. I'm lucky that Alex is willing and able to do it for me, but it should be me up there.

'How long have we got?' I ask him.

He looks at his watch. 'About ten minutes.'

'I'm just going to pop to the loo.'

He squeezes my hand again and smiles in my general direction. He doesn't quite land it and I know it's because he's nervous, even though he's trying hard not to show it.

'I'm going to run out and have a quick smoke.'

I squeeze his hand and we go our separate ways.

The bathroom is huge and white, with fresh flowers on the window ledge and one of those inspirational wooden signs, saying 'Dance like no one's watching'. Really? In the loo? Also, I would hope no one's watching in here.

Of course, they wouldn't be able to see me anyway. One of the best things about being invisible is that I can dance wherever and whenever I want.

I try to pee, but I don't even need to – it's obviously just nerves – so I put the loo seat down and sit and stare at the wall.

I really can't believe I'm not going to get to do the presentation. I've worked so hard on it. The night I walked along the canal and saw the parrot and the giraffe made me realise urban camouflage wasn't the right direction at all. It's about standing out on your own terms. It's about being in control of your image. It's about matching your outsides to your insides. And it's not about blending in or standing out. It's about not feeling invisible.

It's ridiculous it took me so long to work it out, to be honest. But I feel like it's exactly right. It's exactly what Fancy Bantams are looking for. It's exactly what they need. And I want to tell them that myself.

I'm proud of it. For the first time in a while, I'm proud of myself.

I flush the loo, leave the cubicle, and head over to the sink to wash my hands and watch them appear under the water. I turn off the taps and wait for my hands to melt away, but they don't. The water drips off them, but I can still see them. For a second, I'm afraid to look up at the mirror, but when I do I gasp.

I'm back.

CHAPTER TWENTY-NINE

For a few seconds I'm afraid I'm going to hyperventilate. I can't catch my breath. I watch myself in the mirror as my eyes widen, my cheeks flush pink. I reach up and touch my face with my fingers. It's so strange to see myself again. I run my fingertip down my nose and then my thumb across my bottom lip. I close my eyes and open them again, grinning involuntarily when I'm still there. I look down at myself and laugh when I see my body. It's still there. Everything's still there.

'Let me just do your eyebrows,' Tash says staring at me with a slightly wild look in her eyes.

I shake my head. 'No time. And it's fine. No one's interested in my eyebrows.'

I'd dressed nicely just in case – a loose top and wide-leg trousers, and I was even wearing a bra – but obviously I hadn't straightened my hair or put on any make-up. Tash runs a brush through my hair and pulls it into a sort of intentionally messy bun. I'm trying to put on mascara because Tash said the audience won't properly see my face if I don't have any slap on at all. I don't think Alex was planning to wear make-up, but whatever.

I finish doing my eyes and just stare at myself in the mirror a bit more. It's so nice to see my face again. I think of all the years I spent looking in the mirror and picking out the bits I didn't like, the bits I wanted to change. But looking now, I wouldn't change a thing.

'Here,' Tash says. 'Put this on.'

A pinky-red lipstick appears in front of me and I slide it over my lips. I didn't use to wear lipstick much, but it looks good. It suits me.

'Ready?' Tash says.

'Ready.'

As I walk to the side of the stage, Alex turns to look. I see his eyebrows do their thing and then his face splits into a grin.

'Good to see ya,' he says.

He reaches his arms out and I step into them, pressing up against him quickly. I feel him sigh against my neck and then I have to make myself step back. There isn't time.

'You don't mind me doing this?' I ask him.

He shakes his head. 'God, of course not. It's yours.'

'*I'm* yours,' I say, and it doesn't even feel like enough for the way I feel.

He reaches over and runs one finger along my jaw then grazes my bottom lip with his thumb.

'Knock 'em dead.'

I step closer and kiss him quickly on the lips before heading towards the stage.

As the lights go down in the auditorium, I look back at Alex. He grins. Pinky-red lipstick is smeared on his mouth.

I walk out onto the stage. And into the spotlight.

I look around at Trevor, who looks as nervous as I've ever seen him. And Mel, who is staring at me like she can't believe I'm really there. I guess she thought I was going to let them all down. I don't blame her, to be honest.

I glance back at Alex, who gives me a double thumbs-up. I think about the pitch I prepared, but it just doesn't seem right any more. It was right for Alex to pitch for me, but it doesn't feel right for me, here, now. Instead I say, 'I'm going to tell you a story.'

I see Mel roll her eyes, but I take a slow breath and carry on.

'A couple of nights ago, I went to the zoo. It was late, it was dark; I shouldn't really have been there. And I spent some time looking at what I thought was an empty enclosure. And then suddenly, a giraffe appeared. Actually, it didn't appear. It had been there the whole time. I hadn't seen it because it was camouflaged, yes. But also because I hadn't expected to see it. I'd thought the animals would all be inside in their... pens? I don't know if that's what they call them. But because it was night, I assumed the outside part of the enclosure was empty. But then this giraffe stood up – this beautiful creature, like nothing else on earth – and it took my breath away.'

I press my clicker and I know without looking that a photo of one of the Fancy Bantams models, wearing their clothes, leaning against a giraffe, is on the screen behind me.

'I want to talk a bit about what I'm wearing right now, for this presentation. My friend Tash bought me these clothes. She bought them without my input. I didn't even try them on. And I never would have bought them for myself. But look at them. They're perfect. They're perfect because she knows me and loves me and gets me.' I pause, and press the clicker again. 'And also because she's good at fashion.'

The photo behind me is of the Met Gala. Everyone in the shot is wearing brightly coloured, highly decorated, high fashion clothing. But then sitting on the stairs – looking up at Rihanna – is a Fancy Bantams model.

'A different friend told me recently that he likes me for who I am inside.' I glance over at Alex, who looks like he's about to burst with pride. 'Which is a cliché, I know,' I say and he laughs. I look back at the audience and catch the eye of the guy whose office I sneaked into at Fancy Bantams. He's still wearing his beanie, and he's leaning forward in his seat, staring right at me.

'But for reasons that I can't really get into,' I say, 'I believed him. Like Tash, he knows me. He gets me. It doesn't matter to him what I look like or how I dress. He likes me.'

I press the clicker and the picture changes to a photo of a football crowd. Everyone's in team shirts apart from the Fancy Bantams model.

'No one wants to blend into the background all the time,' I say. 'Sometimes, yes. Of course. When it's safer. When you're feeling a bit sad or rubbish or scared. But in the main, I think people want to stand out. But they want to stand out on their own terms. They want clothes that say something about them, that communicate something to other people. We want clothes that express something about ourselves.'

I change to a photo of a Fancy Bantams model standing in the middle of the street in an empty Times Square, the Fancy Bantams logo photoshopped onto one of the bright billboards behind.

I pause. I look at Beanie Guy. At Trevor. At Mel.

'We're all familiar with the expression "Why blend in when you were born to stand out?", right?' I say. 'That's what I think Fancy Bantams needs to show. So far, all of our campaigns have focused on the blending in. I think our new campaign should focus on the standing out.'

CHAPTER THIRTY

Everyone cheers as a glass rolls off the wooden table and smashes on the tile floor.

'Shit,' Tash says.

'I'll get it,' Liam says, standing up and heading over to the bar.

I raise one eyebrow at Tash.

'I know,' she says. 'He's perfect.'

I look at Alex, who grins back at me.

'We had our first row,' Tash says, leaning across the table and lowering her voice. 'He does this weird whisper-shouting thing? It was kind of adorable. And then I was shitting myself 'cos, like, you know, Rob used to say stuff about me being a shrew and I always ended up… just giving in on shit. But we had the row and then he apologised and we fucked and it was brilliant.'

I feel Alex's hand on my thigh and I glance at him. His cheeks have gone pink.

'I know,' Tash says. 'TMI. I'm working on it.'

Liam comes back with another glass for Tash, followed by a barman with a dustpan and brush. I'd half-expected Liam to clean the mess up himself, he's so sweet and earnest, but no. He sits down and drops his arm around Tash's shoulder and then thanks the barman profusely when he's done.

'It is so good to see you!' Tash says, for about the fiftieth time.

I laugh. 'It's good to be back.'

'I just can't get used to it,' Tash says. 'And I can't really believe I managed to get used to… you know.'

'I know,' I say. 'Me neither.'

Because I had got used to it. I was actually happy being invisible. But I think that a lot of the things I enjoyed about it won't go away now that I've 'regained my corporeal form', as Tash once said. I can totally still dance like no one's watching now people can actually see me.

Alex's thumb brushes over the back of my hand and I smile at him again. He can't seem to stop touching me. Or looking at me. From the minute I walked back off the stage, his hands have been on me. And I love it. I would actually have liked to have taken him straight home – for some visible sex – but everyone else wanted to come and celebrate the presentation, so here we are.

Mel is sitting on the other side of the terrace and I think she's already pretty drunk. She came up and congratulated me after the presentation; said she's looking forward to us working together if it all goes ahead. It's going to be interesting. We don't know yet if we get to keep the Fancy Bantams account, but we're all cautiously hopeful – they definitely seemed impressed with my pitch.

'I still can't believe you were really... you know,' Liam says. He's staring at me with a little frown line between his eyebrows.

'I can't either,' I say. 'But it happened.'

'You scared the shit out of me that day,' he says.

Tash laughs. 'It's pretty impressive that you ever wanted to see me again after that.'

Liam stops frowning at me and turns and kisses Tash on the temple. 'I was gone for you from the first time I saw you.'

'Oh shut the fuck up,' Tash says, ducking her head. But she's blushing. Jesus Christ.

'You're very quiet,' I tell Alex.

He shrugs. 'I'm just really proud of you.'

'Oh shut the fuck up,' I repeat, grinning.

*

Trevor comes over, carrying a tray of Jägerbombs.

'Oh god,' I say.

'None of that,' Trevor says. His face is flushed and his shirt untucked, the way it always is when he drinks. 'Everyone's having one.'

Tash and Liam have already taken theirs and I take one and pass it to Alex before taking my own. The four of us clink glasses.

'To having Izzy back,' Tash says.

'To Izzy,' Alex and Liam say.

And then we throw them back.

CHAPTER THIRTY-ONE

Ow, my head. Ow. Ow. Ow.

Ow.

My head.

Why am I even awake? I'm not in work. My alarm wasn't set. Alex is still asleep.

And then I hear it. Someone's knocking at the door.

Fucking hell.

I swing my legs off the bed and then sit up, holding my temples with both hands. God. I cannot believe we drank so many Jägerbombs; they're the fucking worst.

Whoever is at the door knocks again and I say, 'I'm on my way,' but my voice is ridiculously croaky. I cough and for a second think I might actually be sick. I stop in the doorway with both hands over my mouth, but the feeling passes and I manage to get to the front door and open it.

'Izzy?' Jenny, Max's mum, says.

'Hi. Jenny,' I croak.

She looks me up and down and it's only then that I think to check what I'm actually wearing. I look down to see Alex's 'Pokémon Gym Leader' t-shirt. I look back up again. There's nothing I can say about that.

Jenny is, of course, immaculately turned out, as always.

The only thing I can think of to say is, *What are you doing here?* So I don't say anything at all, just take a step back to let her into the flat.

'I'm sure you're wondering what I'm doing here,' she says as she crosses the kitchen and puts her bag on one of the dining chairs.

I blink at her.

'Sorry!' I say, raking my hands back through my hair. 'Sorry. I'm hungover. Do you want a tea?'

'Izzy,' she says. She looks down at my bare feet and then back up at my face.

I feel sure she's here to ask me to take Max back or something equally obnoxious.

'If this is about Max—' I start, but she interrupts me.

'No. No, not at all. Is it okay if I...' She gestures at the turquoise leather jacket she's wearing.

'God, yes, of course,' I tell her.

She takes it off and hangs it over the back of the chair she put her bag on.

'Izzy,' she says again. 'This is really difficult.'

I suddenly think she's about to tell me Max is dead and I lean heavily back against the cabinets.

'Max told us... his father and I... about your money.'

I hear myself make a sound, but I couldn't describe it. I would never have thought for a second that Max would ever tell them.

'Actually, he didn't exactly tell us...' Jenny continues.

Oh.

'Michael... Michael's got himself into some trouble and as a result of that, his father and I have learned things.' She frowns and shakes her head and I suddenly feel horribly sorry for her.

'Sit down,' I say, gesturing at one of the chairs. 'Are you sure you don't want tea?'

'No,' she says, sitting down. 'Thank you. I'm fine. I just need to...'

I nod and sit down in the chair opposite.

'As I said,' she says, folding her hands on the table in front of her. 'Michael has made a mess. I believe that it was originally a sound investment, but… not that that matters now. What matters now is that you are owed a sum of money.'

'Oh,' I say. I'm almost compelled to say something like 'that's okay' or 'don't worry about it' but I bite my lip and keep my mouth shut.

Max's mum lifts her bag off the seat, unzips it, and takes out a cheque book.

CHAPTER THIRTY-TWO

Houghton & Peel are retaining the Fancy Bantams account, but just for this one campaign. If this campaign – *my* campaign – doesn't go well, then obviously they'll be moving to a new agency. It's a huge opportunity for me, as Trevor told me. And Mel told me (through gritted teeth). And I know it is. I've wanted to be a Senior Planner for so long. So why am I thinking about resigning?

I stare out of the train window at the fields racing past and squeeze Alex's hand. He's reading a copy of *Rolling Stone* he picked up at the station, but he puts it on the flip-down table and kisses me on the temple.

'You okay?'

'Nervous,' I say.

'It'll be fine. I'm good with parents.'

I laugh. 'I bet you are.'

'And I bet they're not as bad as you say.'

I laugh again and turn to kiss him. 'They're okay. In small doses.' Very small doses.

I keep thinking about the £7,500 cheque Jenny gave me. And the £2,500 bonus I got for winning the account. I just need to earn enough to cover the mortgage arrears and then I'll be able to do anything I want. It's a scary thought.

And I think about my life before this all happened. How I was just coasting along. I wasn't really happy or fulfilled at work. I certainly wasn't happy or fulfilled in my relationship. Work will be more challenging now. And now I have Alex. But I'm scared I'll slip back into my old routines again.

And Tash is looking for somewhere to live. She's been staying with Liam, but she knows it's too soon to move in with him, as stupidly happy as they are.

'Can I ask you something?' I say, turning in my seat to look at Alex.

He smiles, raising his eyebrows. 'I mean, I don't think it's really the mile high club on a train, but we can give it a go?'

I roll my eyes. 'Not that. I mean... not right now, anyway. I was just thinking... about travelling, maybe. Would you... is that something you might want to do? Again?'

'Travelling?' Alex says. 'With you?'

'Yeah.' My mouth is dry. I take a sip of my cold buffet tea. 'I was thinking that, since I got the Adventure Fund back, maybe I should have an adventure?'

'And you want to have it with me?' Alex says.

'I really do,' I say.

'Then I am all in,' he says. 'And I'll be able to contribute to the Adventure Fund too. If that's okay with you?'

'Of course.' I squeeze his hand. 'How come?'

'Mel's offered me your old job.' He grins.

'Oh my god,' I say. 'That's amazing.'

'Right?'

'Congratulations!'

He dips his head, his hair falling down around his face. I push it back. I love that I'm allowed to do that.

'I was worried you'd be upset. You know, 'cos you thought I was after your job?'

I shake my head. 'God. No. You deserve it. I couldn't have done any of this without you.'

'I'm glad you didn't have to,' he says.

CHAPTER THIRTY-THREE

At Hastings station, Alex goes to get a coffee for me and a green tea for himself while I wait outside for Dad to come and pick us up. I'd said we could get a cab, but he insisted.

It's a hot day – according to the papers, we are about to get a week of sweltering weather – and I'm wearing shorts with high-heeled wedge sandals. That's something else that's changed since I've been invisible: I never would have worn shorts in the UK. I'm anticipating snarky comments from my mum, but she always manages a snarky comment no matter what I wear, so I didn't let it put me off.

A minicab pulls up in front of me and a young guy gets out. He's wearing a football shirt and camouflage shorts. He pays the cab, turns towards me as he heads into the station, and says, 'Alright, hot legs?'

I roll my eyes, glancing back towards the station to see if Alex is on his way out with the drinks. There's no sign of him.

'Hey!' I call after the bloke.

He turns back, smiling, as if he thinks I will have been so bowled over by his charm that I'll offer him a bunk-up in the station loos or something.

'What did you hope to achieve with that comment?'

He frowns, glances down at my legs again, and up at my face. 'What do you mean?'

'You said "Alright, hot legs", yeah? Did you think I was going to swoon? Did you think I didn't know I had legs and you were just being helpful?'

'Calm down,' he says, holding up his hands.

He glances over at the bus queue, where people are clearly starting to pay attention. 'It was a compliment, yeah? No need to get all het up about it.'

'Right,' I say. 'It wasn't, though, was it? It was meant to be intimidating. It's funny how men never pay these compliments to other men.' I see Alex coming through the automatic doors, a cardboard cup in each hand and a bag of crisps in his mouth. 'Oh hey, look! He's got shorts on too!' I'm half-shouting now as Football Shirt gets further away. 'Want to tell him about his "hot legs"? Maybe he doesn't know about them. He'll probably be grateful.'

'Fucking hell,' the bloke says, passing Alex as he heads inside the station.

'What was that?' Alex asks as he reaches me and I take the crisps out of his mouth. 'You okay?'

'I'm fine,' I say, pulling open the crisp bag. 'Oh look. Here's my dad.'

CHAPTER THIRTY-FOUR

'I didn't know Dad knew this many people,' I say as Alex and I walk into the function room of the sailing club.

It's absolutely heaving and I don't even see anyone I recognise. Apparently various aunties and cousins are here, but right now I'm not even sure I'm in the right room.

'Isabel!' I hear my mum shout and I stand on tiptoes and scan the room until I see her. She's up on a raised area, near the windows overlooking the marina. By the flush of her cheeks I can tell she's at least two white wines down.

'Have you seen your father?' she says as Alex and I reach her.

'We just walked in,' I say.

'Well go and wish him happy birthday,' she says, gesturing across the room.

I turn and see Dad standing at the boat-shaped wooden bar. He's got a pint of lager in one hand and what looks like a sausage on a stick in the other. He's talking to three men I've never seen before and he looks happier than I can remember seeing him for years.

'The food's out already?' I say, turning back to look at Mum. She has strict rules on buffets.

She rolls her eyes. 'I know. I said we should wait until later, but he insisted on putting the food out right at the start. Says people like to eat while they drink. I tried to tell him everyone'll be hungry later and it'll be too late, but he wouldn't listen.'

'He looks really happy,' I say. Alex squeezes my hand.

'Oh, he is,' Mum says. I notice she's linked her arm through Alex's – hence the hand-squeeze, presumably – and I grin. Maybe three wines down, then.

'He loves this place,' Mum says. 'Spends all his free time here. To get away from me, I always say. Once he gets the idea to go sailing, it's as if I'm invisible.'

I bite the inside of my mouth. And I daren't even look at Alex.

'You wouldn't know what that's like, would you?' Mum says, bumping me with her free shoulder. 'Not with this one looking all adoringly at you.'

'No,' I say, bumping her back. 'I wouldn't.'

'Your parents are hammered,' Alex says.

'I know,' I say.

They're dancing. Together. I don't think I've ever seen them dance together before. They're both laughing, Dad's twirling her; their friends are clapping along to the music. It's 'Delilah', which I last heard being sung by drunken club-goers in the middle of the night in Camden.

'Do you want to dance?' Alex asks me.

'I don't, actually,' I say. 'I want to go for a walk on the beach.'

We sneak out of the club and walk down the pebbly beach towards the water's edge.

'I love this sound,' I say. 'The water running over the pebbles.'

Alex wraps his arms around me and I rest my head on his chest, looking out over the water, the sky fading violet and peach as the sun sets.

'I think my mum's got a crush on you,' I say.

I feel him laugh into my hair. 'She's out of luck, I'm afraid. I'm all yours.'

'I'm yours too,' I say, tipping my head back to look up at him.
'Ready for an adventure?' he says.
I am.

A LETTER FROM KERIS

Thank you so much for reading this book. I started writing it just for fun and it's probably the most fun I've had writing anything ever. But then every time I told people about it – 'And then she turns invisible!' – the response was 'Ohhh-kay...' I *think* when people read it, they get it...

If you enjoyed it, and want to keep up to date with all my latest releases, just sign up at the following link. Your email address will never be shared and you can unsubscribe at any time. www.bookouture.com/keris-stainton/?title=if-you-could-see-me-now

I really hope you had as much fun reading *If You Could See Me Now* as I did writing it. And if you did, it would be wonderful if you could write a review. And I'm always excited to hear from readers, whether it's via email, on Facebook, or on Twitter (I'll most likely get back to you quickest on Twitter, since I'm there ALL THE TIME).

twitter.com/Keris

www.keris-stainton.com

facebook.com/keriswritesbooks

ACKNOWLEDGEMENTS

Without Kirsty Greenwood this story would be the weird thing I kept re-reading, but never finishing. Thank you for being so supportive and encouraging and hilarious. And for getting me stupid-drunk. Twice.

Huge thanks to my editor Abigail Fenton, who really understood what I was trying to do with this book and sent me edit notes that made me laugh every time. I honestly wasn't sure if I could make the bit of a story I had into an actual novel, and without Abigail I probably couldn't have done.

Thanks to everyone at Bookouture for giving me this opportunity and for making the process so easy and fun.

Thanks as always to my agent, Hannah Sheppard, who didn't even flinch when I said 'I've written this adult thing... It's a bit weird...' Well, maybe she did flinch (I told her on the phone), but she was totally enthusiastic anyway.

Kim Curran gave me brilliant feedback, tips and advice on working in advertising, which made the book so much better. Obviously any and all mistakes are mine. (But Kim *did* tell me artistic license was totally okay...)

Thank you to my lovely writer friends Sarah Painter and Susie Day for reading early drafts and giving incredibly useful feedback. And to David Owen for the 'singing and socks' tweet that inspired Alex's early morning office behaviour.

I also have to thank my amazing WriteWords Chick Lit Group – friends who've been encouraging me since I started trying to write an adult novel (not this one) years and years ago (when we were all still cool with the term 'chick lit'). I'm not going to name them because I'll surely forget someone and that would be bad, but I hope they know who they are. Love you all lots.

And finally to my thirteen-year-old, Harry, for being so keen on the idea of invisible sex that he kept pushing me to finish this book. Sorry, chicken, you're still not reading it.

Printed in Great Britain
by Amazon